Point Horror

THE TRAIN

Diane Hoh

SCHOLASTIC

Scholastic Children's Books,
Scholastic Publications Ltd,
7-9 Pratt Street, London NW1 0AE, UK

Scholastic Inc.,
730 Broadway, New York, NY 10003, USA

Scholastic Canada Ltd,
123 Newkirk Road, Richmond Hill,
Ontario, Canada, L4C 3G5

Ashton Scholastic Pty Ltd,
P O Box 579, Gosford, New South Wales,
Australia

Ashton Scholastic Ltd,
Private Bag 1, Penrose, Auckland,
New Zealand

First published by Scholastic Inc. 1992
This edition published by Scholastic Publications Ltd. 1993

ISBN 0 590 55178 7

Printed by Cox & Wyman Ltd, Reading, Berks

10 9 8 7 6 5

THE TRAIN

Chapter 1

Hannah Deaton surveyed the crowded train station in dismay. Flanked by a pair of friends, she stared at the scene in front of her and thought of an old western she'd seen on television recently. "The cattle are about to stampede," she joked as their small group moved hesitantly forward to join the rest of Parker High School's Teen Tour from Chicago to San Francisco.

The train station was noisy with clusters of students weighted down with backpacks and shoulder bags and suitcases stuffed to excess. Most of the travelers had gathered in groups. Hannah couldn't help feeling sorry for the handful who stood apart from the safety of a cozy, friendly group. Caroline Brewster, a girl in Hannah's geometry class, waited off in a corner by herself, continually glancing at her watch as if she were waiting for someone to join her. Hannah knew she wasn't. She was just pretending.

An unhappy-looking trio caught her attention. Eugene Bryer, a thin, quiet boy with sun-bleached hair and a sullen expression on his pale face, stood off to Hannah's right. With him was Dale Sutterworth, a huge boy with dark hair and glasses, and Lolly Slocum, a stocky girl with sad eyes and lank blonde hair. They weren't talking or laughing as the other groups were, and Hannah couldn't help wondering why they were taking the trip. They didn't seem the least bit interested or excited and she knew they would never be included in the fun.

What was it like to always be on the outside looking in?

Grateful that she and her little group didn't fall into that dismal category, Hannah returned her attention to her own friends and to the excitement of the moment.

The tour's chaperones, two young teachers, Clara Quick and Benjamin Dobbs, stood in the center of the throng, armed with clipboards and looking bewildered. Thirty students were taking the end-of-summer train trip to the West Coast. Ms. Quick, in a pale flowered dress and high heels, and Mr. Dobbs, wearing jeans and a short-sleeved white shirt and blue tie, looked like they'd been slapped with a pop quiz and weren't at all sure they knew the answers.

"Poor Ms. Quick," Hannah murmured. "She looks like she'd rather be home cleaning her oven."

"Yeah," Mack McComber agreed, tossing an arm carelessly around Hannah's shoulders. "I'll bet Dobbs would volunteer to scrub every restroom at school with a toothbrush if it would get him out of this."

"I can't believe we were only allowed one suitcase!" complained Kerry Oliver, who was standing beside Hannah. Kerry was a tall, olive-skinned girl with waist-long, straight black hair that glistened like patent leather. "A whole week on one suitcase? It can't be done. I'll have to wear the same outfit at least twice . . . maybe *two* outfits twice."

The boy next to her gasped in mock horror and clutched at his throat. "Oh, no! Kerry Oliver wearing an outfit more than once?" He was Kerry's height, and stick-thin. A wild jumble of carroty hair threatened to engulf his narrow, tanned face. Warm gray eyes behind wire-rimmed glasses reflected amusement. "Cable cars will stop in their tracks," he teased. "The Golden Gate Bridge will collapse into the Bay. The earth will shake, all because Kerry Oliver could only bring one suitcase to San Francisco."

"Lewis Joseph Reed," Hannah said, her lips curved in a gentle smile, "quit teasing her. We all know you get a kick out of dating the best-dressed girl in school."

"Darn straight!" Kerry said, yanking playfully at a lock of Lewis's burnt-orange hair. "Hannah's right. You love it and you know it. Anyway, don't worry. At least I won't embarrass you on the train by showing up in grubby clothes." Pointing to the bulging maroon bag at her feet, she added, "We're allowed one carry on during the trip." She grinned. "No one said what *size*. Ms. Quick said if we could carry it, we could bring it."

Lewis hefted the bag, testing. He barely raised

it an inch off the tile. Groaning, he glanced around the station before asking, "So where did you park the crane that hauled this over here?"

Hannah laughed.

"Mack will carry it," Kerry said lightly with an unconcerned shrug. She smiled at the tall, husky boy with the dark hair and a strong, rugged face. "He has all those muscles, he might as well use them someplace besides on the football field."

"You must have me mixed up with someone who's all brawn and no brain," Mack McComber said with a grin. "If you think I'm some dumb jock you're going to sucker into carrying that ten-ton piece of baggage you were dumb enough to bring, think again. The rules say, 'if *you* can carry it,' not if someone else can."

Before Kerry could protest, the chaperones, looking grimly determined, took command and began shepherding their charges toward the blue and silver train waiting on the tracks beyond the terminal.

Lewis dragged Kerry's bag, while she danced lightly ahead of him, ignoring his groans. Anxious to get on board the train and "check it out," she hurried ahead, not noticing when Lewis, hampered by the heavy burden, fell behind.

Hannah approached the elephantine coach with mixed feelings. The lure of San Francisco, the city on the Bay, had enticed her into taking this trip. Her parents had visited there several times, and loved it. They assured her she would, too.

But she had been dreading the train ride. Trains

scared her. They went awfully fast, their coaches swaying dangerously as the wheels sped over the tracks. It was a long way from Chicago to California. Was it possible to sleep on a train that was moving so fast and rocking back and forth?

Approaching the steps leading into the coach, Hannah glanced nervously down at the wheels. They were comfortably wide and, made of metal, looked strong enough. But how did they stay on that narrow metal rail when the train reached top speed?

Sometimes, they didn't. She knew that. She had heard about derailments, some almost as devastating as a plane crash. Some people said you were safer on an airplane than you were on the ground.

But this tour had been planned, according to the brochure she'd received in the mail, so that students could "see the country." You couldn't do that from an airplane. So, here she was, at three o'clock on a Wednesday afternoon in late August, boarding a huge, blue and silver train with her friends from Parker High.

Hannah pushed an errant strand of naturally wavy, chocolate-ice-cream-colored hair behind her ears and, urged gently onward by Mack, climbed the steps into the coach.

When everyone was on board, the conductor — a tall, heavy man with a tiny black mustache, and a perfectly pressed blue uniform — led them on a brief tour of the train.

Hannah found it did little to ease her fears. The coaches weren't bad, wrapped in windows that provided lots of light and an all-encompassing view. But the narrow corridors between the sleeping compartments were cramped and dark. The walls were covered with a dark paisley print of rust, deep gold, and navy blue. The carpet underfoot shared the same gloomy pattern. Hannah felt a grim, heavy feeling descend upon her each time they entered a new car.

Mack noticed her nervous shivers. "You cold?" he asked with concern.

Hannah shook her head. "No. It's just . . . nothing. Never mind." She wasn't about to let a silly case of jitters spoil Mack's fun. *He* wasn't afraid of anything. At least, she didn't think he was. She'd only gotten to know him about six weeks before, in the middle of summer. But she'd never seen him frightened. Maybe that came with his size. What would anyone so big have to be frightened of? While she, on the other hand, barely came up to Mack's armpit and weighed only ninety-six pounds, soaking wet.

Shaking aside her gloomy feelings, Hannah continued onward with the group. But she let Mack fold her hand inside his, telling herself it was so they wouldn't become separated as Lewis had, struggling somewhere behind with Kerry's bag.

The Cafe, Hannah decided upon seeing it, was a fun place. No dark paisley here. Instead, the walls were panelled in a warm, light wood, and the stools, tables, and booths were a vivid red. Skylights and windows made it feel light and airy. A cheerful tune played in the background while passengers separate from the Teen Tour sat at the bright-red Formica counter sipping cold drinks.

Everyone wanted to order something to eat or drink, but Ms. Quick insisted they "get settled first." A special low tour rate had allowed the students to be housed in compartments rather than coach, which Hannah appreciated. She and Kerry would have more privacy in a compartment. And Kerry had insisted that she never could have slept in "one of those chair-beds. I need to lie *down* to sleep!"

Lewis met them in the corridor. He was empty-handed and he looked worried.

"Where's my bag?" Kerry asked him immediately, her eyes going from one of his hands to the other. "Did you put it in your compartment?"

Lewis shook his head. Rusty strands fell against his forehead. He shoved them back nervously. "No . . . I . . . the conductor made me stow it in the baggage car, Kerry."

Kerry shrieked.

"He said it was too big to be a carry on. I argued with him," Lewis added desperately, seeing the flush of anger begin on Kerry's face, "but it was no go. He just took it from me and headed for the baggage car. But," he added hopefully as Kerry drew in a breath in preparation for another shriek, "the baggage car isn't locked. You can go get what you need from your bag."

"Lewis," Kerry cried, her cheeks deepening in color, "my *face* is in that bag! And most of my clothes for the trip!"

Lewis frowned, uncomprehending. "Your face?"

But Hannah understood. Kerry's makeup and hair care supplies were in that bag. Kerry would have to boomerang back and forth between their compartment and the baggage car every time she wanted to change her "look." Which, knowing Kerry, would be often.

Hannah knew Kerry wouldn't accept this arrangement.

She didn't. "This is ridiculous!" Kerry said, turning away from Lewis. "Ms. Quick said we could have a carry-on bag and that's what I brought! Who does that conductor think he is, anyway? Lewis, you have to go get that bag. I *need* it!"

"Kerry," Hannah offered, "you can share my stuff."

Kerry stared at her. "*Your* stuff? Hannah, you only wear mascara, and you use that cheap stuff. It gives me a rash."

Hannah flushed and fell silent.

"Lewis?" Kerry turned a stern gaze on her boyfriend.

"Look," he said, "I told you, you can go get what you need when you need it. Quit making such a big deal out of it. The conductor said you can't have that bag on the train, so live with it."

Kerry's mouth fell open. Then, just as quickly, she clamped it shut. She turned to Mack. "Mack?"

He shook his head.

"All right. All *right*!" Kerry said grimly. "I'll get it myself. I need that bag, it's mine, and I have a right to have it with me."

And, swinging her black hair angrily, she stomped off down the corridor, heading for the baggage car.

She was back only minutes later, before Hannah, who had gone into their compartment, had had time to open her own small tote bag.

Kerry pushed the compartment door open and immediately sank into one of the seats. Her face was an odd pea green, her dark eyes wide.

She did not have the carry-on bag.

"What's wrong?" Hannah asked. "Did the conductor yell at you?"

Kerry shook her head. "No," she said almost in a whisper, "I didn't even see him. But Hannah . . . Hannah, you won't believe what's *in* there. You won't . . ."

"In the baggage car?" Hannah smiled. "Luggage, I guess."

"It's not funny," Kerry snapped, surprising Hannah. Hannah took a couple of steps forward and sat down beside her.

"Kerry, what's the matter? Why are you acting so weird?"

Kerry lifted her head and looked straight at Hannah. Then she said with horror, "Hannah, there's a *coffin* in the baggage car!"

Chapter 2

"*A coffin?*" Hannah repeated in response to Kerry's grim news.

Kerry nodded. "Yes. In the baggage car. It's sitting up on a table that's draped with a long black cloth." She shuddered. "A coffin! A *dead* person is on this tour, Hannah! It's disgusting."

Hannah sat in thoughtful silence for a moment and then said, "Kerry, maybe there isn't anyone *in* it. Someone along the train route could have ordered a coffin from Chicago. You know . . . someone from a little town where they don't *have* coffins. So they have to send away for them when someone . . . dies."

Kerry sent her a skeptical look. "Hannah, how can a town not have coffins? One thing people do absolutely *everywhere* is *die*. Even the tiniest town would have to have a funeral parlor, and funeral parlors have coffins."

Hannah wasn't ready to surrender. "Well, maybe someone's relatives didn't *like* the coffins in their town, so they sent away for a fancier one. Someone with a lot of money . . . that's possible, right?" She paused, and then added, "I'll bet there isn't anyone in that coffin. It's just an empty box, Kerry. So quit worrying."

Who are you trying to convince? she wondered. Kerry or yourself? Hannah tried never to think about dying, or dead things. They frightened her. Maybe that was childish, but she couldn't help it.

Kerry shivered. "I've never been around anyone dead before. Gives me the willies."

Hannah nodded. "When I was six," she said, the words dragging with reluctance, "my grandmother died. I went to the funeral parlor with my parents. They didn't make me do anything gross like kiss my grandmother when she was in the coffin, but I hated being there. Everyone kept saying how natural she looked, how peaceful. But she didn't. I stayed overnight with her lots of times when I was little and she'd fall asleep in her chair while we were watching television. She looked peaceful then. But in her coffin, she looked . . . mad. Like . . . like she hadn't been ready to die."

"Hannah, cut it out! You're giving me the creeps!" Kerry sat up straighter. "I think we should go find out if someone is in that coffin."

Hannah drew in her breath sharply. "You're kidding, right? You'd better be."

Kerry stood up, tossing her black hair as she always did whenever she changed positions. "If I'm going to have a good time on this trip, I have to be sure that coffin is empty. You should want to know, too, Hannah. We do *not* want to share this tour with a dead body. Besides," Kerry added, "every time I want something from my bag, I have to go into the baggage compartment to get it." She shuddered again. "I couldn't stand it if I knew a corpse was in the room with me."

Hannah knew what Mack would have said. He would have said, "Kerry, don't you *get* it? A person inside a coffin can't possibly hurt you. You couldn't *be* any safer."

Hannah didn't say that, because she shared Kerry's uneasiness. Maybe it was silly — Mack would say it was — but she couldn't help the way she felt.

"I'm not going with you," she announced as firmly as her voice would allow.

"Oh, yes, you are!" Kerry grabbed Hannah's hand and pulled her up out of the seat. "I'm not going in that room alone. You're my best friend, Hannah Deaton. You wouldn't want me to worry through this whole wonderful trip, would you?" Kerry's voice changed from one of command to one of pleading. "C'mon, Hannah! I'm sure you're right. The coffin is probably empty. We'll just pop in, I'll grab a white sweater from my bag, we'll see if there's a tag on the box, and once we know for sure that it's just an empty coffin, we'll head for the Cafe and some fun."

"What if — what if it *isn't* empty?" Hannah asked. "It's not like we can do anything about it."

Kerry's mouth tightened. "It *will* be!"

The train began to move then, catching them by surprise. It moved slowly at first, making its way out of the station, and then quickly picked up speed.

It was surprisingly quiet, Hannah thought, and there was less movement than she'd feared. The cars didn't sway back and forth as if they were getting ready to tip over. Beneath her feet she could hear the wheels. They didn't make the loud, annoying clackety-clack she'd expected. Instead, the wheels provided a steady but muted background sound, a soft, constant *ga-dink*, *ga-dink*, *ga-dink*.

Kerry sighed impatiently.

Hannah wished fervently that she could believe her own theory about the coffin being empty. But she knew people were often shipped back to their hometown for burial in a family cemetery plot. No matter how many years they'd spent in other places, they wanted to be buried close to where they'd been born. It seemed odd to her. It wasn't as if they'd *know* . . .

Stalling for time, she said, "Kerry, how are we going to know if the coffin's empty without opening it?"

"New stuff that's being shipped to somewhere else has an invoice taped to it," Kerry told her knowingly. "I had to push aside a whole bunch of boxes to get to my bag. The boxes all had invoices wrapped in plastic taped to the side. If you're right about the coffin being shipped empty, it'll have one of those invoices taped to it."

Hannah nodded. "And if I'm wrong?" she couldn't help asking as Kerry reached for the handle on the compartment door. "What will the tag say then?"

Kerry shook her head. "Don't think about it. I refuse to accept the possibility. Come on."

As they left the compartment and entered the corridor, Hannah felt her stomach begin to churn. She hated and feared small or narrow spaces. The dark walls and floor seemed to press in on her, cutting off the light, as if she were walking through an airless underground tunnel.

By the time they reached the baggage car at the far end of half a dozen coaches, Hannah was having trouble breathing.

"What's the matter with you?" Kerry asked as she pushed the heavy door open and peered inside. "You're wheezing. You sound like my brother when he has an asthma attack."

"Claustrophobia," Hannah answered with difficulty. "There's not enough room. . . . I feel closed in, and I hate it."

"You'll feel better in the Cafe," Kerry said confidently. "It's lighter and brighter and there's room to move around. This'll just take us a minute, then we'll head for the bright lights, the music, and the fun." Kerry lowered her voice to a whisper. "Now where are the lights?"

There were no windows in the baggage car. "Wasn't it dark when you were here before?" Hannah asked.

"No. The light was on. C'mon, help me find the switch."

After several moments of creeping around in the dark, Kerry found the switch and flicked it on. A lone ceiling fixture cast eerie shadows over their faces and over the long, narrow room half-full of suitcases, boxes, crates, and cartons.

Hannah spotted the coffin right away. It was, as Kerry had said, on a long, narrow table that was covered with a floor-length black cloth. Although Hannah's eyes immediately darted over every inch of the wooden box's surface, she saw no sign of an invoice, and her heart sank.

Closer examination confirmed that there was no invoice. The coffin was not empty.

In the chilly, shadowed room, Hannah and Kerry stared at each other with dismayed faces.

"Look," Hannah finally said, her voice not as steady as she would have liked, "we're being silly. Nothing in this room can hurt us, Kerry. Let's just get out of here."

"No, wait! There's a tag, there, on the corner." Kerry hesitated, clasping her hands together and then, before Hannah could stop her, she lunged forward to read the small, square white tag hanging at one end of the coffin.

"Kerry, let's *go*!" Hannah cried. An overwhelming sensation of dread began to sweep over her like a chill fog. She began backing away, her eyes fastened in morbid curiosity on Kerry, bending to read the tag.

"Oh, my God!" Kerry bolted upright and turned to face Hannah. Her hands flew up to cover her mouth and her skin became gray.

Hannah, watching, saw the scene in slow-motion. "What?" she whispered, continuing to back away, "what's wrong?"

Kerry opened her mouth, but no sound came out. She tried again, sidling sideways away from the coffin.

"Hannah," she said hoarsely, "it's someone we *know*. Knew. I never thought it would be someone we *knew*."

Confusion flooded Hannah's face. "But . . . but no one we know died, Kerry. No one."

Kerry nodded grimly. "Oh, yes, someone did, Hannah. Don't you remember? *Frog* died."

Hannah frowned. "Frog?"

Another nod. "Yes. The tag on the coffin has his name on it. Frederick Roger Drummond. On its way to San Francisco, where his parents live."

Speechless, Hannah stared at the coffin.

Kerry did the same. "Hannah that's . . . "

Hannah finished the sentence for her. "That's Frog in there."

Chapter 3

In the stunned silence that followed, the steady *ga-dink, ga-dink, ga-dink* of the train wheels racing along the rails seemed to send Hannah a warning: *Go-back, go-back, go-back* . . .

But we *can't* go back, she thought as she reached out to clutch Kerry's hand. They won't take the train back to the station just because Kerry and I don't want to travel with . . .

"How could they put it on this train?" Kerry cried, still staring at the coffin. "It's just not *right*! Why didn't they put it on a regular train with people who never knew Frog? Why did they have to put it on this one and ruin our trip? It's not fair!"

"I don't know," Hannah whispered. But the part of her that hadn't been shocked senseless pointed out silently that maybe there wasn't a lot of choice when it came to shipping a body. You probably couldn't sit around and wait for a particular train. Arrangements would have to be made, grieving relatives would be waiting . . . you probably had to use the first train that was going in the right direction.

Would there be grieving relatives for Frog? There would have been for her: her parents, her younger brother, Tad, her grandfather. Even her parakeet, Disraeli, would miss her and probably wouldn't eat for a while. Kerry, too, had parents, grandparents, cousins. And Mack and Lewis had tons of friends and relatives who would mourn if anything terrible happened to them.

But Frog? Did he have anyone? In California or anywhere else?

He must, or he wouldn't be on his way west.

But it was hard to imagine.

"Do you think Lolly and Eugene and Dale know Frog is on the train?" Kerry whispered. "He was their best friend. They never went anywhere without him. That's creepy."

Was that why the trio had looked so glum in the terminal, Hannah wondered? Because they knew Frog's coffin was on the train?

"Maybe there's a memorial service in California. Maybe they're going for that."

"Let's get out of here," Kerry said finally, breaking the silence. She began backing away, as Hannah had earlier, as if turning her back on the coffin would be inviting trouble. "Let's go tell Mack and Lewis."

"They won't care. They'll think we're silly for getting upset. They'll say Frog can't hurt anyone now, so why let it bother us that he's on the train? That's what they'll say."

* * *

Hannah was right. That was exactly what the boys said.

They were in the Cafe, sitting with Jean Marie Westlake, a red-haired girl who had once dated Mack. Hannah felt no pangs of jealousy upon seeing the two together. That was history and, besides, Jean Marie was too nice a person to flirt with someone else's boyfriend.

Hannah quickly glanced around. She saw no sign of Lolly or Eugene or Dale. But the backs of the shiny red booths were very high, hiding people from view.

"You will never," Kerry breathed as she and Hannah slid into the booth occupied by their friends, "guess what's in the baggage compartment. Never!"

"Baggage?" Lewis quipped, sliding over to make more room. Mack started to laugh, and then caught the expression on Hannah's face.

"What's wrong?" he asked her quietly, and Jean Marie looked at Hannah with concern in her eyes. "Are you sick?" she asked. "You look like you've seen a ghost."

"That's what I'm trying to *tell* you," Kerry said. "Not that we've seen a ghost," she added hastily, "but it's almost that bad." She took a deep breath and exhaled before saying dramatically, "Frog's coffin is on this train!"

"Yeah, I know," Mack said calmly. "I was out there when they loaded it on the train."

Hannah looked at him sharply. "Why didn't you say anything? Maybe if we'd known ahead of time . . ."

"Sorry." Mack shrugged. "It's not the kind of thing you bring up in ordinary conversation. It would sound pretty weird to say, 'Hey, let's have a good time on this trip — even though Frog's coffin's on board.' "

Kerry sent him a disgusted look. "You wouldn't have had to say it like that. But you still could have told us. I can't believe you didn't say anything."

"How would I know you were going to pack your entire wardrobe in a carry-on bag? Is it my fault you have to run back and forth to the baggage car every five minutes?" Mack asked. "I never expected you or Hannah or anyone else to know the coffin was there. So why would I mention it?"

"I don't see what the big deal is," Lewis said to Kerry. "The guy is dead. Burned to death when his car hit that wall. It's not like he's going to be bugging you during the trip."

"Lewis!" Hannah cried. "That's gross!"

Jean Marie nodded. "He was only seventeen, Lewis. What happened to him was horrible. I know he wasn't very nice, but nobody deserves to die that way." She paused, and then added, "My dad said the firemen worked for forty minutes to get him out of that car. It was twisted like a pretzel and they couldn't open the doors. Then it burst into flames — " She stopped, so appalled by the image that she couldn't continue.

"I know he lived with his grandmother," Hannah

said, feeling better now that Mack's safe, solid bulk was there beside her, close enough that she could feel its warmth, "but he must have family in California." She glanced around the table. "He wouldn't be on the train if there wasn't someone there, waiting . . ."

"His parents," Jean Marie offered. "They couldn't cope with him, so they sent him here, to live with his grandmother. But . . . she had a heart attack right after Frog's accident. She's in the hospital."

"They dumped him?" Lewis said, incredulous. "His folks dumped him?" Lewis's own parents were fiercely proud of their son, and would have fought anyone who tried to take him from them.

Hannah didn't blame them. Lewis was neat. A great kid. Not at all like Frog . . .

"You know, my mother works in the school office," Jean Marie said. "Well, she said his records showed that he skipped school a lot in California and he was picked up by the police a couple of times for stuff like speeding and shoplifting. I guess his parents got tired of the hassles, so they shipped him here."

They all fell silent then, thinking about Frog.

After a few moments, Mack said slowly, "I remember the first class I had with him. Bio. He showed up in December, right before the midterms. Here was this big, hulking kid with long greasy hair and bad skin and anyone could see he had an attitude problem, and here he was coming in in the middle of the year — social death for a junior in high school. Everyone checked him out real quick and then wrote him off, know what I mean?"

They all nodded silently. They knew.

"Brutus" — Mack's nickname for their biology teacher — "told him to write his name on the blackboard. Frog made a face, but he did it. When he went up to the board, everyone could see his jeans were filthy and he hadn't shaved in a couple of days." Mack grinned slightly. "And we're not talking fashion statement here, guys. He just didn't *care*."

More nods. Whatever it was that Frog *had* cared about, it hadn't been his appearance.

"He wasn't poor," Kerry said. "His grandmother had money . . . that big house and a new car every year. He didn't have to be a slob." There was awe in Kerry's voice as she tried to comprehend appearance not being important to someone.

"Anyway," Mack continued, "Frog started to write his name, Frederick Roger Drummond. He never used the Frederick, so he wrote the initial F, then R-O-G. And when he got that far, I yelled, 'Hey, the guy's name is Frog! ' " Remembering, Mack flushed with shame. "I don't know why I did it. It was a rotten thing to do. But some guys wouldn't have minded. If Frog had laughed, maybe everyone would have liked him even though he looked pretty scuzzy, and things would have been different. But he didn't laugh. Everyone else did, though. And the name stuck."

No one said anything. Hannah told herself Mack hadn't meant to be cruel, but she couldn't help thinking what it must have felt like to Frog, being the target of everyone's laughter on his first day at Parker.

"I keep seeing his face when he finished and turned away from the blackboard," Mack added, his voice quiet and serious. "He looked like he was going to explode: red face, eyes popping, fists clenched . . . like he wanted to smash someone's face in. Mine, I guess. Every time I passed him in the hall after that, he looked at me like he'd love to crush me under the heel of his boot."

Another long silence passed, broken only by the carefree sounds from other tables, where no one was thinking of a dead boy or a coffin.

Finally, Kerry spoke up. "You weren't the only one who was mean to Frog," she said, her eyes on the bright red tabletop. "I was, too."

Then she fell silent.

Chapter 4

When Kerry didn't elaborate, Lewis volunteered, "Don't waste time on guilt, Kerry. I don't think anyone at Parker qualifies for the Be-Kind-To-Frog award." He glanced around the table, mild annoyance on his face. "But what good does it do Frog to spin your wheels feeling guilty now?"

Kerry flushed an unhappy scarlet. "I didn't *say* it did any good! I just meant, after seeing that . . . coffin . . . I couldn't stop thinking about what I did to him."

"It couldn't have been anything so terrible, Kerry," Hannah said loyally. "You're not a mean person." She meant it. Kerry was spoiled and a little shallow, but she wasn't mean.

"Before he started dating Lolly Slocum," Kerry said, "Frog asked me out."

Lewis laughed out loud, and Mack whistled.

"It's not funny! He made me mad right at the start, acting like he was doing me a favor. Strutted right up to me, hands in his pockets, the whole macho routine." She made her voice go very deep.

"Hey, babe, how about a movie tonight?" Kerry sighed. "I've never been rude to boys, even when I couldn't stand them. I know it's hard for them, never knowing if they're going to be shot down when they ask a girl out. So I try to be nice when I say no."

"You weren't that terrific when I asked you out the first time," Lewis teased. "You said you had to wash your hair. We all know what *that* means. It means you find us totally repulsive."

Kerry didn't laugh. "I *did* have to wash my hair. Anyway," she added crossly, "you were just too sure I'd say yes. That bugged me."

"If you were nice to Frog when you turned him down," Jean Marie said, "you don't have anything to feel guilty about."

Kerry lifted her head. "But that's just it. I *wasn't* nice! He was so creepy-looking. Something about his eyes. They were empty — nothing there, you know? And I don't think I ever saw him smile." Kerry shuddered, remembering. "When I said no, I couldn't go out with him, he actually *argued* with me. He asked me why I wouldn't, and I gave him some stupid excuse like I had to go shopping with my mother or something, but he still didn't leave. He said he was as good as anybody else at Parker and if I didn't give him a really good reason why I'd said no, I'd be sorry."

Hannah gasped. Frog had threatened Kerry? "You never told me that, Kerry. Why didn't you?"

"I forgot about it. Really."

"So far," Lewis said, "I haven't heard word one

about how you were mean to Frog. Sounds to me like it was the other way around."

"I laughed at him." Kerry shifted uncomfortably in her seat. "He made me so nervous, making this big fuss right there in the hall with a whole bunch of people around staring at us, that it was either laugh or cry. I look awful when I cry, so I laughed."

"*Now* I hear mean," Lewis said grimly. "Something every guy lives in terror of is being shot down with *laughter* when he asks a girl out."

"I *know* that, Lewis!" Kerry cried. "And I'd never, ever done it before. And I'll never do it again. The look on his face . . . it was like you said, Mack — like he wanted to strangle me, right there in front of everybody. It made my blood freeze." She frowned. "I never could understand what Lolly saw in him. She was so quiet, like she was afraid of her own shadow, and Frog . . ." Kerry fell silent.

No one said anything, and after a minute or two of silence, Kerry added, "I knew it was rotten to laugh at him. And now he's dead, and I can't tell him I'm sorry."

"Would you have if he'd lived?" Lewis asked pointedly.

Kerry thought for a minute and then said softly, "No. I guess not."

"Then quit thinking about it now when it doesn't do any good."

Hannah was surprised by his tone of voice. It wasn't like Lewis to be unsympathetic, especially with Kerry.

She learned why a moment later. Lewis sank

back in the booth and let out a long breath of air. "Okay," he said, his mouth tense, "since this seems to be true confession time, and since Kerry seems determined to beat herself up as if she were the only person in the world who eighty-sixed Frog, I don't mind admitting that she *wasn't*."

"I know that, Lewis," Kerry said quietly. "Nobody liked him. Except for Lolly — and Eugene and Dale. And that was only because they didn't have anyone else."

"I didn't just dislike him," Lewis persisted. "I got him kicked out of gym class."

Surprise flooded Kerry's features. "You did? Really?" She knew, as did Hannah and Mack and Jean Marie, that Lewis brought home every stray animal he came across, had once torn down his treehouse and rebuilt it elsewhere because it was interfering with the home of an owl and its family, and coached Little League baseball during the summer. If Lewis had a mean bone in his body, it was well-hidden.

But Lewis nodded. "I was captain of one of the basketball teams in gym when Frog showed up. Coach told me to pick him, so he'd feel at home." Lewis shook his thatch of rusty hair. "But the guy looked like he had two left feet, and I had a bet with Mack that my team would win. Anyway, I knew if I picked the new guy, we'd lose. We had a good chance against Mack's team, but putting that Neanderthal on the team could have screwed things up. So I gave Coach a hard time about it. And Frog heard us arguing."

Hannah listened silently. Her stomach was churning again. She told herself it was from the gently rocking motion of the train as it sped along the tracks, but she didn't quite believe it. Was that really it? Or was it because they kept talking about Frog? She knew *he* couldn't hear them. Hannah glanced around nervously. She wouldn't want Frog's friends overhearing this conversation. It would upset them.

"I remember that day," Mack was saying to Lewis. "Frog's first day in gym. And he wasn't the only one who heard you, Lewis. We *all* heard you. When you get excited, your voice really carries."

Lewis nodded in agreement. "I know. I guess I got carried away. Didn't even think about how the guy might be feeling if he overheard me. Geez, why didn't you stop me, Mack?"

Mack leaned back against the booth and laughed. "Are you kidding? You were on a roll, Lewis. There's no stopping you when you get wound up like that."

"Also true. Anyway, the guy heard me and stomped over. Started calling me names. He got madder and madder and when it looked like he was about to take a swing at me, Coach kicked him out. Sent him to Decker's office."

Decker was Parker High's vice-principal. No one liked him, possibly because he was an effective disciplinarian.

"I heard later that he suspended Frog for two days," Lewis added, his voiced edged with regret.

"A crummy way to start school in a new place, right?"

Hannah thought so. But she said nothing. Lewis was feeling bad enough.

"If you were the one who was arguing with Coach," Jean Marie asked, "why weren't you kicked out of gym, too?"

"Because he's a varsity basketball hotshot," Mack said with a sardonic grin. "Coach is no fool. He *needs* Lewis this season. He knew he didn't need Frog. You could tell just by looking at the guy that he'd be a disaster out on the floor."

"That shouldn't have mattered," Jean Marie argued. "Coach should have given Frog a chance. And so should you, Lewis."

He didn't argue with her. There was a bleak expression on his face that made Hannah want to reach out and pat his hand. But she said nothing. All she wanted now was a change of subject.

"I'm starving!" she announced, although the very thought of food made her ill. "Let's order something to eat, okay?"

But, lost in guilt, Lewis and Kerry shook their heads silently and Jean Marie said, "He came into the journalism office, too, asking if he could be a reporter."

Jean Marie was the editor of the *Parker Pen*, the school newspaper. "I took one look at him and knew I couldn't use him." Her hands, wrapped around a glass of soda, tightened until the knuckles turned white. "It was so unfair of me. I never even asked him if he'd worked on a school newspaper before or if he was interested in writing. I just told him, flat out, that there weren't any openings for reporters. I said they'd all been assigned at the beginning of the year, and he was too late."

"Well, that's true, isn't it?" Kerry asked.

Jean Marie shook her head. "No, it's not. Students can come in any time and sign up. And Frog probably found that out soon enough. He would have figured out then, if he hadn't earlier, that I just didn't *like* him."

After another long silence broken only by the train wheels whispering to Hannah, *Go-back, go-back, go-back*, Kerry turned to her and said, "Hannah? You're the only one who hasn't said anything. Wasn't Frog in your English class? Did you ever talk to him? What I really want to know is, did you make him mad like the rest of us? What's *your* story?"

"I don't have one," Hannah replied. Then saying, "Excuse me," she slid past Mack and out of the booth to hurry to the counter.

"Well!" Kerry cried, offended.

Hannah ignored her. She didn't turn around in an effort to make amends. She stood stiffly at the counter, her back to her friends, listening as the train wheels repeated their warning.

Go-back, go-back, go-back . . .

Chapter 5

Hannah stood at the counter, alone, sipping the Coke she'd ordered. Laughter and music and chatter surrounded her, but she heard only the warning of the wheels telling her to go back.

Everyone seemed so happy. The Cafe was cheerful and lively in its coat of bright red, and sunshine and light streamed in through the windows and skylights. Each round red table, every booth, was occupied by a group of four or five laughing, joking students, every bright red stool filled, and the upbeat music inspired more than one foot to tap out the beat on the red-and-white checkered floor tiles.

So much life here. But at the other end of the train, in the baggage car . . . there was a coffin.

Go-back, go-back, go-back . . .

She couldn't go back any more than Frog could. Frog — Frederick Roger Drummond — dead at seventeen, killed in a horrible, fiery crash not far from her house. They heard the sirens, she and her friends, and had dismissed them. Busy, she thought, we were busy and we paid no attention.

Not that they could have helped. Jean Marie had said the car was a blazing mass of melting metal when help arrived.

Poor Frog. Kerry had said, "He shouldn't have been going so fast. He always drove too fast. He almost hit me once, roaring out of the school parking lot. I screamed at him, but he didn't hear me."

But Frog couldn't have known that on this particular Friday night, driving too fast was going to kill him. If you were only seventeen and you knew absolutely, positively that something was going to take away the rest of your life, you wouldn't do it, would you? Not even if you were unpopular and unhappy, like Frog. Not at seventeen. Not unless you didn't want to live anymore.

Could Frog have been *that* unhappy, that night? Guilt and shame washed over her. Could she and her friends have made the new boy so miserable that he would actually end his own life?

We didn't mean to, she told herself quickly to ease the pain that washed over her. We didn't *mean* to. We didn't know.

But the police hadn't mentioned suicide. No one had. She was imagining things. A guilty conscience . . . ?

"Penny." Mack came up behind her, startling her out of her morbid thoughts.

Hannah looked up at him. "What?"

"I'll give you a penny if you'll tell me what you're thinking about. My grandmother used to do that, offer me a penny for my thoughts."

Hannah smiled. "A penny won't even buy chewing gum now, Mack. Inflation. You'd better up the price."

"Okay, a nickel then, but that's my top offer."

"I was thinking about Frog," she answered reluctantly.

"Don't."

"I can't help it. Everyone talking about him just now . . . we really weren't very nice to him."

"Hannah, he was a creep. Don't make him a saint now because something awful happened to him."

"I'm not." Hannah's tone was more defensive than she'd meant it to be. She wanted Mack to understand what she was feeling. But how could he? None of them had liked Frog, that was the truth, and Mack was being more honest about it than she was.

Still, she couldn't shake the eerie feeling that Frog was listening to every word she said. The thought raised the flesh on her arms in tiny bumps.

"Hannah and Mack," Kerry cried, "come on back here! Lewis is telling incredibly stupid jokes and if you don't get on over here, he'll keep it up. Save me!"

Hannah turned, Coke in hand and, at that instant, without warning, the cheerful light allowed by the huge windows and the ceiling skylights disappeared as the train entered a tunnel. A split second later, the overhead lights went out, and the entire Cafe was plunged into total darkness.

There were screams and voices saying, "What the . . . ?" Hannah clutched for Mack's sleeve. The utter blackness, combined with the hollow sound of the train rattling through the tunnel, made her breath catch in her throat. She hated tunnels. There was no way out of them — you couldn't just decide halfway through, I don't like this tunnel anymore, and leave it by a side exit. There was only the entrance and the exit, and some tunnels were very, very long. There was no space, no air, and you were surrounded on all sides by concrete or rock. Sometimes there was water above and on both sides of the tunnel, and Hannah found those the scariest of all. Did this train go through that kind of tunnel? She didn't know.

Why had the Cafe lights gone out?

The screaming and shouting was followed by a bewildered, shocked silence. Into it rang Ms. Quick's voice. "All right, everyone, calm down! You've been in darkened rooms before, and you survived."

Her weak attempt at humor fell flat. When no one laughed, and a few boys yelled complaints, Mack calmly asked the chaperone, "Any idea what the problem is? We know the tunnel is dark, but what happened to the lights in here?"

"I don't know," Ms. Quick answered, her voice close enough to Hannah that she thought she could probably reach out and touch the teacher if she chose. She didn't. Mack's sleeve was enough for now.

A startled gasp came from somewhere off to Hannah's left. She peered through the darkness but could make out only the bulky shadow of a booth.

The train left the tunnel as suddenly as it had

entered, and natural light and sunshine flooded the Cafe through the skylights and windows.

Ms. Quick went immediately to the light switch on the wall beside the entrance to the Cafe and flicked it, bathing the already bright room in artificial light.

"Well, honestly!" the teacher exclaimed in disbelief, "someone turned off the switch!"

When she realized that no one was listening to her, she clucked in annoyance. Then her eyes followed theirs, and she gasped in horror. Everyone in the Cafe was staring in mute shock at Lolly Slocum, sitting alone in a bright red booth off to Hannah's left.

Hannah thought, Did she hear all the things we said about Frog?

And then the horror of the scene before her obliterated all thought.

What everyone was staring at was a bright red print bandana, twisted into a "rope" and wound around Lolly's neck so tightly that her round, plain face was rapidly turning purple and her eyes, wild with desperation, were bulging dangerously. Her fingers clawed frantically at the brightly-colored noose, but in vain. Her mouth opened and closed silently as she struggled for precious air.

Like a dying fish, Hannah thought numbly.

Lolly Slocum was choking to death.

Chapter 6

While everyone watched, transfixed, Mack took two huge steps forward and began working on the bandana knot digging into the back of Lolly's purple neck.

A waiter whispered, "What should we do?"

The elderly man working behind the counter gave no response other than to continue staring, wide-eyed, at the victim.

"Someone get the conductor!" Ms. Quick barked. "See if there's a doctor on board!"

Lewis whirled and ran.

The only sound in the room as Mack struggled with the stubborn knot was the ugly, tormented gurgling coming from Lolly Slocum.

This isn't happening, Hannah thought, sickened by the sight of Lolly's bulging eyes rolling back in her head. This can't be happening. It can't be real.

"I think she's had it," someone said softly, eyes on Lolly. Then someone else said, "Well, who *is* she? Is she with our tour?"

The question saddened Hannah. Lolly's fellow students didn't even know who she *was*. Parker High wasn't such a big school. Shouldn't they all know each other? Shouldn't the people watching Lolly fight for her life at least know who she *was*?

When at last the bandana gave way under Mack's fingers, Lolly took one deep, grateful gasp of air, and fainted. Her head fell forward like a sack of sand. There was a loud, sickening thunk as her forehead slammed into the red Formica tabletop.

Several girls screamed.

"She's dead!" one cried, and then the same voice asked tremulously, "*isn't* she?"

Ms. Quick checked Lolly's pulse. "She's alive. But she needs a doctor. *Where* is Lewis with that conductor? Oh, I do hope there's a doctor on board."

There was. A tall, gray-haired woman in a dark suit arrived with Lewis and the conductor. She was carrying a fat black bag. Lolly was beginning to stir, moaning hoarsely, when they burst into the Cafe.

"Everybody out!" the doctor snapped, hurrying over to help the victim sit up. Singling out an adult in the group, she turned to Ms. Quick and added, "Except you! I want to know what happened here."

With the doctor's help, Lolly leaned her head back against the seat, her mouth working furiously to gulp in air. An ugly necklace of raw, wounded skin encircled her throat.

Flushing guiltily, Ms. Quick waved everyone else out of the room. "Go straight to your compartments and stay there until you hear from me," she ordered in a shaky voice. Then she turned her attention to doctor and patient.

Shock slowed the steps of the tour group as they left the Cafe. "Is that girl going to die?" someone whispered as they made their way through the cars.

"I don't think so," Mack said. "If she was, she probably wouldn't have regained consciousness."

That remark broke the stunned silence. Everyone began talking at once, some softly, some more loudly, about what had happened to Lolly. There was disbelief in every comment.

When the door had been closed and latched from the inside, the compartment felt safe. But Hannah knew that Lolly's attack had changed the tour for all of them. Looking at the pale, drawn faces of her friends as they collapsed onto the maroon velour seats, she knew they were still seeing Lolly's mottled, swollen face.

"You think she'll live?" Lewis asked Mack, his voice subdued.

Mack shrugged.

"I keep seeing her face," Kerry said, leaning her head back against the seat and closing her eyes. "It was . . . it was awful." She trembled. "Horrible!"

"It must have hurt," Hannah whispered, sitting down beside Mack. "She looked like she was in such terrible pain. Who would . . . ?" She couldn't finish the question, but they all knew what she had been about to say.

Who would do such a terrible thing?

Kerry opened her eyes. "Maybe one of those

weirdos she came with did it. That Eugene character was Frog's best friend. Maybe he freaked out and decided Frog wants Lolly with him. I've heard of weirder things."

Mack and Lewis clucked in disgust.

But Hannah remained silent. Once, when she had visited her grandmother's grave in the cemetery, she had come upon Eugene, sitting with his back against a tree. Thinking he was there for the same reason she was, she had said politely, "It's kind of nice that we can bring flowers here. I think it sort of helps, don't you?"

And he had looked at her with pale, cool eyes and said, "I just come because I like it here."

Hannah found herself wondering how Lolly had ended up with three such strange boys as her only friends. Unlike Frog, Lolly wasn't really unattractive. She was a big girl, but it seemed to Hannah that she at least made an effort to look her best, wearing neat, clean clothes, trying to jazz them up a little with a colorful scarf around her neck or a pretty pin on a blouse collar. Hannah remembered seeing her once in the hall in a plain, short-sleeved white blouse, a small bunch of artificial violets pinned to the collar, repeating the color of the purple corduroy skirt Lolly was wearing. She had looked almost pretty.

So it wasn't appearance that had set Lolly apart. And it wasn't attitude, the way it was with Frog. Lolly Slocum was pleasant enough in classes and in the halls, nodding or smiling at people she passed.

"Why don't any of us like Lolly?" Hannah asked

quietly as Mack and Lewis, Jean Marie and Kerry continued to sit in shocked silence. Their faces were still gray with shock and disbelief.

Kerry stared at her. "What?"

"Why isn't Lolly more popular? Most of the people in the Cafe didn't even know who she was. I mean, she seems nice enough. So why doesn't anyone like her?"

"Because she dated Frog," was Kerry's immediate answer. "And Frog was a creep."

"No, I mean, *before* that. Before she dated Frog. Why didn't we like her then?"

Her friends exchanged confused glances. Kerry shrugged. "How should I know? I don't remember. I think . . . I think she was just . . . not *fun*. Too . . . quiet or something. What's the difference, anyway? Even if we *had* liked her, when she started going out with Frog we would have changed our minds, right?"

"Maybe if we'd liked her," Hannah said slowly, "she wouldn't have gone *out* with someone like Frog. Maybe she wouldn't have had to."

Lewis groaned. "More guilt? Look, some sick nut turned off the lights and wrapped a noose around that girl's neck. But it didn't happen because of the way we treated Frog or his girlfriend Polly."

"Lolly," Hannah said, agitated. "Her name is *Lolly*."

"Actually," Jean Marie said, "it's Louise. Her real name is Louise. She was in Choir, and Mr. Foley called her Louise."

"I didn't know she was in Choir." Hannah

frowned. "Did you ever talk to her, Jean Marie?"

A pink flush of shame colored Jean Marie's cheeks. She shook her head. "No, not really. But," she added quickly, "she was only there a couple of times. Then I guess she quit, because all of a sudden, she didn't show up. Foley was really mad. She had a nice voice. Alto. We're short on altos. I heard she'd joined the Drama Club instead."

A sudden rap on the door ended the conversation about Lolly. Startled, they all stared at each other and no one moved.

Chapter 7

"It's me!" Ms. Quick's voice called from beyond the door. "Let me in!"

Hannah jumped up and opened the door.

The teacher stood in the hallway. "Lolly is going to be all right," she said, relief in every syllable. "The doctor said she could continue the trip, but we're having trouble calming her down, and she wants to go back home. I can't blame her. We're sending her back on the express train."

I want to go, too, Hannah thought. I want to go back home.

Ms. Quick glanced around the room. There was dismayed awe in her voice as she said, "Isn't this the most awful thing? I can't believe . . ." Then she took a deep breath and said in a monotone, "I want you all to stay here until it's time to go to the dining car for dinner. No running around the train alone, not until we find out who's behind this horrible business. Dr. Lindsay has volunteered to return to Chicago with Lolly so that Mr. Dobbs and I can stay with all of you."

"So what happens next?" Mack asked.

"We're asking everyone on the tour if they have any idea who might have done this. They've all said no. What about you five — any ideas?"

They all shook their heads.

"Well, then, since no one knows anything, the conductor will be calling in a detective to get some answers. He'll come on board first thing tomorrow morning when we arrive in Denver. Until then, I must urge all of you to please stick together, okay?"

They all nodded solemnly, and Ms. Quick left to continue spreading the news.

Thoroughly shaken by the disastrous way their trip had begun, they all sat quietly, gazing out the window at the speeding landscape and the rapidly descending twilight.

It was ten minutes past eight o'clock when Ms. Quick rapped on the door and said it was time to head for the dining car, reminding them once more to "stay together."

The thought of eating dinner turned Hannah's stomach. But the others eagerly got up to go. "I need to stop back at our compartment first," Lewis told Mack. "Need anything there?"

"I'd better come with you. I think Ms. Quick is right. We shouldn't be wandering the train alone. Not after . . ." Mack didn't finish the sentence. "I guess two qualifies as a group. Let's go."

"Walk me back to my compartment?" Jean Marie asked. "Sherry and Ann are probably already there. I can go to dinner with them, but I don't want to walk back there alone."

The three left together, with Lewis and Mack promising to return to go with Kerry and Hannah to dinner.

A few minutes later, the train slowed gradually and came to a complete standstill. Hannah went to the window and watched as Lolly, flanked by the doctor and the conductor, was helped out of the tour train and into a red and silver train standing at the station and aimed in the opposite direction. As she watched the unfortunate girl collapse into a seat in the well-lighted train, Hannah couldn't help thinking she looked relieved. She's *glad* to be off our train, glad to be going back home.

No wonder, after what had happened to her.

Was it really safe to wait until morning and let the detective figure things out?

It didn't feel safe. How could they be sure that Lolly's attacker had left the train?

They couldn't.

Dinner in the dining car would be creepy, Hannah thought. Everyone would be watching everyone else, trying to decide if anyone looked suspicious. There wouldn't be any laughing, the way there had been in the Cafe earlier, and if people talked about anything at all, it would be the attack on Lolly.

Hannah didn't want to go to the dining car. But anything was better than staying in the compartment alone. That, she could *not* do.

Soon they were on their way again, the wheels droning their steady *ga-dink, ga-dink, ga-dink.*

Go-back, go-back, go-back . . .

Hannah turned away from the window. "It was

nice of the doctor to go back with Lolly. So she won't be alone."

"Yeah, but what if she was the only doctor on board?" Kerry asked. "Let's just hope nothing else bad happens. I hope whoever was after Lolly knows she's not on *this* train anymore." Kerry pulled the barrette out of her hair and then replaced it carefully. "I wonder who it was? Why would anyone want to kill Lolly Slocum?"

She means, Hannah thought with sadness, that Lolly wasn't interesting enough or important enough to have something like that happen to her. How awful. Hannah sighed, and slowly began to unpack her small suitcase.

Chapter 8

It seemed to Hannah that it was taking Kerry forever to get ready for dinner. Mack and Lewis came to get them twice. Both times, Kerry sent them back to their own compartment, insisting that she needed a few more minutes. They left grudgingly.

"Kerry," Hannah finally said, "you've changed your hair four times. After what's happened, how can you stand there fussing with your hair as if life were totally normal? It's *not*."

But, in truth, she was grateful. . . . The thought of leaving the safety of the compartment for those dark, narrow corridors made her palms sweat. There would be no bright sunshine relieving the darkness now. The windows and skylights would reflect only empty darkness. The corridors would seem airless, confining . . .

"You're right, Hannah. I'm being petty and shallow and silly." But in the next second, Kerry peered into the mirror over the small sink and cried, "Look at this purple eye shadow. Purple! I feel like a peacock. Wait just one minute, let me try this beige.

The salesgirl at Bonham's talked me into the purple. I could strangle her."

The word "strangle" hung in the air and Kerry's eyes widened as she realized what she had just said. "Oh," she said softly, glancing guiltily at Hannah, "sorry. I wasn't . . ."

"It's all right. Just hurry up, okay? Mack and Lewis must be starving. If you send them away one more time, they'll go without us." And I don't want that, Hannah added to herself. I definitely don't want that.

The minute Kerry finally finished primping, she became impatient. "Where are those guys, anyway?" she complained. "I've been ready for five minutes and they're still not here. Let's go get them."

Lolly's swollen, purpled face danced before Hannah's eyes. "You know what Ms. Quick said. And you *told* the guys to give you more time. They'll be here. If we leave first, we could miss them."

"Hannah. There is only one way to get from their compartment at the other end of the car to ours. It's not like the train has side streets. C'mon, we'll surprise them. It'll be fun."

"No. Ms. Quick said — "

"Hannah, the guy who tried to throttle Lolly left the train when she did, I'm sure of it. Why would he hang around here?"

"Okay," Hannah said, "you're right. We'll probably run into Mack and Lewis on the way."

But as they left the compartment, her stomach began churning again. The corridor was so dark, and completely empty. Kerry had taken so long making herself beautiful that everyone else had already left for the dining car.

They had gone only a few steps when Kerry let out a piercing shriek and stopped in her tracks.

Hannah gasped and whirled, expecting to see a crazed maniac holding a knife against her best friend's throat.

"I forgot my gold chain," Kerry cried. "The one Lewis gave me for my birthday. I never go anywhere without it. I promised him I wouldn't. But I took it off when I was brushing my teeth because it kept dangling over the stupid little sink and I didn't want to get toothpaste gunk all over it. Wait here. I'll be right back."

"I am not waiting in this hall alone," Hannah said, "and do not ever, ever shriek like that again on this train!"

"Sorry. It was dumb. You okay?"

"Yes. But I'm coming with you."

"Hannah, don't be silly." Kerry was already backing away. "Our compartment is only a few inches away. I'll be right back. I know exactly where my chain is. And Mack and Lewis should come along any minute now."

Their compartment was more than "a few inches" away. More like a few *hundred* inches. But Hannah *did* feel silly refusing to wait alone in the corridor. Hadn't she already decided that Lolly's attacker had left the train when Lolly left?

"Okay," she agreed, "but hurry up. Are you *sure* you know exactly where that chain is?"

"Of course I do. Wait right here. Back in a sec."

And Kerry hurried away, her black hair swinging behind her like a pendulum.

The minute Hannah stood alone in the corridor, lost in a sea of dark paisley, her nerves tightened like piano wires. She couldn't help it.

The train wheels whispered, *ga-dink*, *ga-dink*, *ga-dink* . . .

When Kerry didn't return immediately, Hannah, restless and impatient, moved on down the hall to the door at the end of the car. Its window looked out upon a dark, moonless night, but in the distance, lights appeared and disappeared, blurring into one, long, pale gold ribbon. The black and gold panorama was hypnotizing and Hannah became lost in it, unaware of the passing minutes.

A sound behind her snapped her out of her trance.

"It's about time," she said, as she began to turn around. "Couldn't you find the chain?"

Without warning, something thick and fluffy and cottony covered her mouth and nose, stifling her cry of surprise.

A strong arm fastened itself around her chest, pinning her arms against her sides. The arm began dragging her backward, her legs dangling helplessly. She fought to touch the ground with her feet, but when she did, the only result was the sound of her sneakers hitting against the dark carpet.

Help me! Hannah tried to cry out, but her mouth, mashed cruelly into the cottony fluff, made no sound.

And it occurred to her dazed, terrified mind that even if she could scream, there was no one to hear her.

The corridor was empty.

Snapping out of her paralysis of fear, Hannah began to fight back. She tried frantically to slow their progress by digging her heels into the carpet, but the soft rubber soles of her sneakers were useless. Her attacker plodded onward, toward the baggage car. Hannah's desperate attempts at resistance seemed to go unnoticed.

Why hadn't Kerry returned? Hannah wondered. She had said, "Back in a sec." She'd been gone much longer than a second. Much longer . . .

She heard the door to the baggage car slide open.

If only someone . . . a porter . . . the conductor . . . someone was in the baggage car to help her.

Hannah realized they had moved inside the car. A booted foot pushed the door closed. Hannah's eyes, seeking help, darted wildly about the room.

There was no help. There were only boxes and cartons and containers, which offered no help at all. There was no porter, no conductor . . . no one to help her.

They shouldn't leave all this luggage unguarded, she thought angrily, crazily. When I get out of here, I'm complaining to the conductor.

Complain? I'm losing my mind. I probably won't even get out of here . . . alive.

Lolly's tomato-hued face danced before her, and nausea rose in her throat. Calm, calm . . . must stay calm . . . mustn't panic . . . must think . . . think . . . think . . .

Think, Hannah! Think or die!

How could she think when she was so scared?

Because she was being dragged backward by the grip around her chest, she couldn't see where they were headed; which only made her feel more helpless.

Who was this person dragging her along? And what were they planning to do with her? Was she going to die here?

Suddenly, the dragging stopped and the hand that was gagging Hannah removed the cottony wad over her mouth. Stunned by the unexpected release, Hannah found herself standing upright, freed from her awkward backward-tilt. But her arms were still imprisoned.

Immediately, she opened her mouth to scream for help.

The blow came from behind. Hannah never saw the arm descending, never saw the blunt object that slammed against her skull, sending a sickening shaft of pain zig-zagging, like lightning, from the top of her head all the way down to her toes.

No scream left her lips. Before any sound could escape from her open mouth, darkness swooped down upon her.

Chapter 9

Hannah awoke into a blackness that was as thick and cloying as tar. Her eyes, aching from the blow on her head, searched for the tiniest sliver of light, and found none. She closed her eyes again, hoping that when she opened them, the darkness would be gone.

It wasn't. Wherever she was, there wasn't so much as a pinprick of light. She felt like a mole burrowed into the deepest part of the earth.

Her head hurt terribly. Sharp shafts of pain stabbed at her skull. She put her hands, unfettered now, to her forehead. They were cool, almost clammy, but soothing. Slowly, maddeningly slowly, her mind returned to full consciousness.

Where *was* she?

She was lying flat on her back, legs stretched out, on something soft and silky . . . so slippery that when she tentatively bent her leg at the knee and slid it up toward her, her sneakered foot promptly whooshed back into a flat position again as quickly as if she were lying in melted butter.

She raised the other leg. But this time, she didn't bend it at the knee. Instead, she lifted it higher and higher, testing, until the foot touched something, some kind of cover over her head — over her body — over all of her. The cover felt very solid. Maybe . . . wooden. She pushed against it with her foot. But the wood covering her remained firmly in place. There was no "give" to it. She pushed hard, then harder still, using all of the strength in her legs. But whatever was lying over her, covering her in the dark, was solid and thick and . . . sliding her hands over it . . . wooden. Satin-smooth wood. Thick . . . solid . . . totally immovable wood.

Where *was* she? What was she doing in all this cold blackness?

She raised both legs and pushed once more against the overhead surface with all of her strength.

Nothing. The wooden covering remained firmly in place.

Hannah's left arm moved away from her forehead to reach out to the side. Another solid surface, this one close, very close. *Too* close.

Her nerves began to sing out an alarm as her right arm followed the motion of her left, sliding along her right side until she touched solid wood. Again, too close . . . no more room than a few inches on either side.

Not enough space . . . too narrow . . . something solid over her head and on both sides of her, keeping her in . . .

Not enough room . . . not enough space . . . not enough air . . .

Hannah's breathing began to quicken, coming in shallow little gasps.

Easy, easy, she warned herself. Don't panic. Do *not* panic. Take it easy. Find out where you are, that's the first thing.

What *was* this place? Why was she lying down? Had she fainted? No, she never fainted. Sometimes, when claustrophobia hit her in an elevator, she hyperventilated, but she never fainted.

Her head throbbed. She remembered, then, being struck on the back of her skull. Whoever had done that had put her in this . . . this place. *Why?* And how could she get out when the top wouldn't budge?

Her hands moved more quickly now, seeking, searching for the key to freedom, a way out so that she could begin to breathe normally again. So small, this place . . . so small, so narrow, so dark. Hannah knew in her heart that it would only be seconds before she panicked in earnest. It wasn't as if she could help it. It wasn't something she chose to do, breathing erratically in small, confined spaces. She always tried to fight it, but it was no use. And now her breathing was already out of control, and unless she found an escape soon, her heart and lungs would begin to careen around in her chest on a wild rampage.

If she only knew where she was, maybe she could find a way out.

Forcing herself to take a few slow, deep breaths,

she slid down on the silky fabric underneath her, until her feet touched another solid surface. Then, pushing against that "wall" with her sneakered feet, she slid her body back up, arms at her sides, until the top of her head gently bumped into more solid wood.

She did this twice, sliding to one end of the darkness, then back up to the other end, her hands exploring the smooth wooden sides as she went, until she had a clear picture of the dimensions encasing her in wood.

And that picture, when it was complete in her mind, caused her breath to catch in her throat. Her chest began rising and falling far too rapidly as Hannah realized that she was lying in a long, narrow, wooden box with an unyielding wooden roof. No windows, no doors, not nearly enough space or air. Where was the way out? Her hands continued to flutter about, touching . . . exploring . . . sliding along the slippery folds of the melted-butter fabric under and around her.

It felt like . . . it felt like . . . satin.

Hannah's breathing quickened. She scrambled upward, slamming the top of her head against the heavy wooden cover. She cried out in pain. A lid . . . the wooden cover over her head was a . . . lid. She was in a long, narrow wooden box with a lid, and she was lying on . . . folds of . . . satin . . .

Her eyes, in the darkness, widened and her mouth opened. No . . . nononononono . . .

Her grandmother's funeral zoomed, unbidden, into her mind — Nanny lying there in that long, narrow, wooden box, the curved lid raised so that everyone could see her artificially made-up face, lying there, unmoving, on folds of rippled . . . white . . . satin—

Oh, God, no . . . No!

Hannah opened her mouth and screamed and screamed and screamed . . .

Her head tossed crazily from side to side. Her fingernails began clawing and scratching and tearing at the solid wood surrounding her. Finding no escape, her screams escalated to high, thin, keening wails . . . the wild cries of a newly caged animal.

Her legs thrashed frantically, slamming repeatedly against the lid of her prison. Her hands dug and clawed, searching for a way out. Her breathing became so shallow and rapid, there was no air left for screaming, and her wailing descended into a guttural, pained moan.

Hannah fought to remain conscious. But she was hyperventilating, and purple and red dots danced before her eyes.

When she heard voices, she thought she was hallucinating. Using what little strength she had left, she lifted her legs and slammed her feet against the lid hard, once, twice, three times.

Then, telling herself the voices weren't real, Hannah gave up the fight and passed out, sliding down along the white satin with a sob and letting the blackness swallow her up.

Chapter 10

When Hannah struggled back to consciousness, it took her some moments to realize she was free. Out of the horrible box — free! Someone was holding her. . . . Mack . . . Mack was holding her in his arms, her face against the softness of his flannel shirt.

Hannah's eyes struggled to focus. Slowly, the milky cloudiness disappeared as realization dawned. As it did, the sensation of being trapped in the long, narrow wooden box returned in vivid detail. Hannah began shaking violently. Covering her eyes with both hands, she began to moan.

"It's okay, Hannah, it's okay," Mack murmured. "You're out of there now, you're safe, it's okay." None of which did any good. Hannah continued to writhe and moan.

Lewis arrived with Ms. Quick in tow, followed closely by the conductor. Their faces registered hope that Lewis's jumbled story involved only a cruel prank, a joke.

That hope vanished when they saw the state Hannah was in.

"Goodness!" the teacher cried, hurrying to Mack's side. "*Look* at her! This is *not* funny!" She fixed a steely gaze on Mack. "What's been going on in here?"

"Someone shut her in there," Mack said, pointing to the now-closed coffin. "We'd been hunting all over the train for her. This was the only place left to look, and Kerry thought she heard something when we first came in here. It stopped right away. Hannah must have passed out. But we had to check it out."

Ms. Quick paled. "Hannah was in *there*?"

Mack nodded grimly. "And she's claustrophobic. That's why she's so out of control. She needs a doctor." He looked at Lewis. "Did you find one?"

"Aren't any," the conductor offered, his eyes on Hannah, whose moans had dwindled into a soft, anguished sobbing. "Only doctor on board left with that other girl. We have a first-aid kit, but," he shook his head ruefully, "I don't think there's anything in there for this kind of thing. Girl needs a sedative. Calm her down. She's in a bad way."

"You would be, too," Kerry spoke up, "if you'd been trapped in someone's coffin."

The conductor nodded. "Might be I could find a tranquilizer, something like that, on board. Passengers might have something. Want me to ask?"

"No," Hannah whispered, lifting her head and surprising all of them. "I don't want any pills." Thin streaks of watery mascara veined her bloodless skin and her eyes were red and swollen. But her breathing was steadier and she tried to sit up in Mack's arms. "Someone hit me on the head. When I woke up . . ." she shuddered, "I was . . . in *there*."

She stopped to take a deep breath. "Whoever did it is probably still on the train. If he . . . if he comes back, I don't want to be asleep from some pill." She made no attempt to leave Mack's arms. "I want to be able to defend myself," she added in the same hoarse whisper.

"You won't have to," Mack said. His voice was full of determination. "I'll be here."

"Someone struck you?" Ms. Quick asked in a shocked voice. "Then this wasn't just a stupid joke?"

"If it was a joke," Lewis said, "it's not funny. Not funny at all."

"It wasn't a joke," Hannah said softly. "I was waiting for Kerry in the corridor and someone grabbed me from behind and dragged me in here. Then something slammed against the back of my head. The next thing I knew, I was . . ." she swallowed hard and continued in barely a whisper, "in there."

"Did you see who it was?" Lewis wanted to know.

"No, I didn't see anything," Hannah said. "I told you, he came from behind. Can I go back to my compartment now, please? I need to . . . I need to wash my face. I . . . I need to . . . sit down or something."

"I'll take you," Mack said. "Come on." But before

they left the baggage car, he turned to Ms. Quick and asked, "So what are we going to do about this? Hannah could have died in that . . ." — he couldn't bring himself to say coffin — ". . . in there. We have to *do* something."

The teacher nodded. But it was clear that she was at a loss, still shocked by what had happened to Hannah.

"Serious business," the conductor said glumly. "That detective is meeting us in Denver, first thing tomorrow morning. Have to leave it to him to find out what's going on."

"I guess we'll have to." Mack's arm around Hannah's shoulders tightened. "We'll look out for each other until the guy gets here."

"You're sure this wasn't a crazy kind of stunt?" the conductor pressed. "Bunch of kids on a train trip, high spirits, that kind of thing?"

The teenagers shook their heads vigorously. "No joke," Lewis said, "absolutely."

The conductor nodded, and left the car, shaking his head as he went.

Ms. Quick was shaking her head, too, and her expression clearly said, How did I get myself into this? But she was concerned for Hannah, too, and followed closely behind Mack as he led Hannah from the car.

Hannah's mind whirled in confusion. She had been in a coffin. Frog's coffin. But there was something very, very wrong with that, something more than the awful horror of her imprisonment. There shouldn't have been room for her in that awful box.

Coffins weren't made for *two* people. Only one person . . . one body.

What had happened to the body that was supposed to be in the coffin? Where had it been while she was struggling so hard to get out?

Where was Frog?

Chapter 11

"You need a doctor," Ms. Quick told Hannah, as she and Mack helped her to one of the seats. "Your color is very bad."

"I'll see a doctor in Denver in the morning," Hannah said, closing her eyes again. "But not tonight. I just want to sleep. I'm so tired."

"Hannah," Kerry said suddenly, "your hands . . ."

They all looked at Hannah's hands. Every nail was torn, many of her fingers were bloody, the knuckles scraped raw.

Kerry ran to the sink and quickly wet a washcloth with cool water. Returning to Hannah, she knelt and carefully, gingerly, began wiping the wounded hands clean. Each time Hannah winced in pain, Kerry did the same. "I'm sorry." She said it several times. "I'm really sorry it hurts."

But when she had finished, Hannah's hands felt better, and she said so with gratitude in her voice.

"I hate to leave you," the teacher said. "You will lock your door?"

"We'll be fine," Hannah assured her. "All I want to do is sleep. Kerry, you're staying, right?"

Kerry nodded. "I wouldn't leave you here alone, Hannah."

The boys offered to stay, too, but Ms. Quick nixed that idea. They left reluctantly, especially Mack. Hannah promised him she would sleep, but he still looked worried as he stepped out into the corridor.

"Close your eyes," Kerry commanded gently as she released the upper bunk and climbed into it. "You don't want that doctor in Denver finding you a total wreck and shipping you back home like Lolly, do you?"

Hannah wasn't sure. In spite of her uncertainty about the safety of rail travel, she had looked forward to this end-of-the-summer excursion with her friends. She had been especially excited about seeing San Francisco. But now it looked like train travel could be dangerous in more ways than one. And where did you run to on a train when you were in trouble? There wasn't any place to *go*! You were trapped . . .

When Hannah was twelve, her family had moved from the small town in Idaho where she was born to the suburbs where they now lived. To her dismay, she'd suddenly found herself traveling to and from school on a big yellow bus. She was the only "new kid" in the area that year, and still had braces and wore glasses. She'd been teased unmercifully, made the butt of everyone's jokes for weeks until she was no longer so "new" and they'd accepted her.

But while it lasted, the worst part of all that misery had been the fact that there was no way to escape. There was no place to run to on a school bus, no place to hide. She'd had to sit there and take it, fighting tears of loneliness and pain until suddenly, for no apparent reason that she could see, it ended and she became one of them.

What she felt now, huddled on her bed shrouded in the blanket, was that same sense of trapped-animal fear. If she continued with the trip as planned, how could she feel safe again? Where could she hide? Where could she run to if she was attacked again?

Only a lunatic would jump from a speeding train.

Maybe she should give up now, while she was still in one piece, and go back home. I never thought I would envy Lolly Slocum, she thought, but I do now. I want to be safe, too.

But . . . something in Hannah bridled at the idea of some hateful, crazy person she didn't even know driving her away from the tour, scaring her away from her friends and her trip. That wasn't fair. It wasn't right.

She had her friends around her, and Ms. Quick and Mr. Dobbs, and soon the detective would arrive.

She was staying on the train. She would be very, very careful, but she was staying. For now, anyway.

Exhausted, aware that the door was locked and Kerry was close by, Hannah fell asleep.

* * *

When she awoke the following morning, the first thing she heard was the whisper of the train wheels: *Go-back, go-back, go-back.*

No, she thought clearly. No, I won't go back. Not yet, anyway.

On the bunk above, Kerry hadn't stirred. It was too early to get up.

I should go back to sleep, Hannah thought. I'm still tired. And I want that doctor to think I'm in good shape so he won't send me back home.

Going back to sleep was easier said than done. Thoughts of Frog, unbidden, crawled furtively into her mind . . . first on the edges of it and then, when she was unable to resist, into the middle of it, taking up every inch of her thinking space. Because . . .

Because where *was* he? If he'd been in his coffin where he belonged, there wouldn't have been room for *her*.

The idea that someone might actually have moved Frog's remains made her physically ill.

What kind of person would do such a ghastly, disgusting, horrific thing?

Well, then, where *was* he?

Hannah was reminded of her mother's standard comment whenever Hannah misplaced something: a sneaker, her locker key, a favorite sweater . . . "Well," her mother always said, "it couldn't get up and *walk* away."

Neither could Frog. Not now. Not ever again.

Unless . . .

The thought came into Hannah's mind like a snake slithering through deep grass, arching its narrow head to snap, sending its venom coursing through her veins. The stunning, incredible thought stabbed her, venom-like, with a sharp and wicked pain.

No — impossible! How could she even think such a thing?

But . . .

Frog had burned to death. How many times on television had someone supposedly burned to death in a car or plane crash and then turned up alive later? Happened all the time, didn't it? It always turned out that someone else had died in the character's place and no one suspected.

Could someone other than Frog have died in that crash?

Who? A hitchhiker? Had Frog stopped to pick up someone that night — some innocent person wandering the highways — just before the car crashed? Had Frog himself escaped a split second before the wreck burst into flames? No one would have checked the identity of the driver. No dental records would have been examined. The police would have assumed that, of course, it was Frog driving the car. They had no reason to think anything else.

Hannah bit her lower lip. No. It couldn't be. It was too bizarre. It was *Frog's* car that had crashed and burned. Frog would have been driving it, so Frog would have died . . . no question about it.

But if that were true . . . Frog would have been in the coffin. And he wasn't. Hannah was.

He's here, she thought clearly, her head snapping

up so suddenly she smacked it against the upper berth. He's *here*. Somewhere. And he's . . . he's *angry*.

We shouldn't have been so mean to him, she thought, her heart slamming so wildly against her chest she expected Kerry to lean over the upper bunk and cry, "What's that horrible noise?"

But Kerry slept on.

Frog is out to punish us, Hannah thought with sickening conviction. Those stories we all told in the Cafe . . . they were awful. Cruel. He's not going to let us get away with that.

But Hannah, the nasty little voice reminded her slyly, *You* didn't *tell* a story. You were the only one who made no confession. So why would Frog be out to punish *you*?

For that matter, an even bigger question was, Why would he want to hurt Lolly? Lolly wasn't part of Hannah's group. She was Frog's own girlfriend.

I *know* what we all did to Frog, Hannah thought. But what was it that Lolly did to make him angry enough to hurt *her*?

A sharp rap on the door interrupted Hannah's thoughts.

"Time to get up, girls!" Ms. Quick's voice called. "Denver in an hour." Then, "Hannah? Are you awake? How are you feeling?"

"I'm okay," Hannah answered, forcing a casual tone of voice. Why worry Ms. Quick? She was frantic enough already.

Besides, Hannah could just imagine the look on the teacher's face if she knew Hannah thought Frog was alive. The woman would have a stroke and the whole trip would be cancelled.

Maybe that wouldn't be such a bad idea.

Hannah didn't say anything about Frog being alive to Kerry, either. What if Kerry thought Hannah had freaked out completely because of last night? She couldn't stand the thought of Kerry looking at her as if she had left her mind behind in that coffin.

Besides, saying it aloud would make it so . . . *real.* And now that it was daylight, now that she was washing her face and combing her hair and slipping into a pair of jeans and a red long-sleeved sweatshirt, now that Kerry was up and chattering about how "totally starving" she was, thoughts of Frog being alive seemed *Twilight Zone*-ish.

An hour later, she had convinced herself that her morbid thoughts about Frog had been irrational. Because she felt safe with Ms. Quick at her side as they waited at the doctor's office in downtown Denver, she insisted that Mack go with the others to eat breakfast in a nearby restaurant.

"You'd be bored waiting here for me," she told him, "and I'm not the least bit hungry. I couldn't eat anything. Go ahead."

"I don't want to go until I'm sure you're okay," he argued, lingering by her side.

"Mack," she said with a wan grin, "Go eat! I'll wait for you here when I'm done with the doctor."

Mack finally agreed, and left with Kerry, Lewis, and Jean Marie. Hannah's expression was wistful as she watched them troop off down the street. If it hadn't been for last night, she'd be going with them on this crisp, clean morning in Colorado, having the time of her life instead of waiting to see a doctor.

The doctor gave Hannah a clean bill of health and some aspirin for her headache.

As they left his office, Ms. Quick said, "You know, Hannah, if you want to return home, we can put you on a train to Chicago this morning. If that's what you want."

"No," Hannah said, recalling her resolution from the night before not to let some crazy person force her off the trip. "I'll stay."

"All right," Ms. Quick said, as she and Hannah waited outside in the sunshine for Hannah's friends to appear.

Other students, checking out Colorado's capital city, passed them. Several threw curious glances Hannah's way and she realized the word was out. News of the attack on her had been making the rounds. She hated that. It was humiliating.

Dale Sutterworth and Eugene Bryer, looking odd without Lolly walking between them, passed by.

Eugene looks mad, Hannah thought as his eyes briefly met hers and then quickly moved elsewhere. Was he still angry about the attack on Lolly? Having no one but gloomy Dale as a traveling companion couldn't be much fun.

A little while later, Kerry and Lewis came sauntering up the street with Jean Marie tagging along behind, studying the storefront windows.

But there was no Mack with them.

He's late because he's ordering take-out coffee for me, she told herself even as her heart began pounding in her chest.

"Where's Mack?" she asked and to her surprise, the words sounded perfectly normal.

"Not here yet?" Lewis asked, surprise on his face. "That's weird. When we came out of the restaurant, we started to head this way and all of a sudden, Mack yelled something and took off down the street. We figured he'd decided to jog or run back here, maybe for the exercise. Then," he added with a grin, "we figured, he'd been away from you for more than five minutes, and was feeling Hannah-withdrawal pains, so he decided to race back here to relieve his symptoms." The grin disappeared as Lewis frowned. "But he's not here. That's weird. Where could he be?"

Hannah sucked in her breath. When she spoke, her voice was little more than a whisper. "I don't know," she said. "I don't *know* where he is."

Chapter 12

"Perhaps Mack misunderstood," Ms. Quick told Hannah. "He might have thought he was supposed to meet you back at the train. Why don't we go back there?"

"He promised to meet me here. And that's what he'll do," Hannah insisted. "I'm waiting."

Realizing that there was no changing Hannah's mind, and anxious to return to her other duties, Ms. Quick volunteered to return to the train station to see if Mack had arrived there. "Don't wait too long," she warned before she left. "The train will be leaving as soon as that detective arrives."

Hannah knew the train would never depart without all of its Parker passengers. Ms. Quick would lie down on the tracks, if necessary, to prevent that.

And it didn't matter, anyway. Hannah was far more worried about Mack than she was about being stranded in Denver.

She turned to Lewis. "Why did you let Mack leave like that?"

"Like I could stop him," Lewis replied drily. But

his gray eyes searched the avenue for any sign of his best friend. "I told you, he just took off. He acted like a man on a mission. If we had a clue about what that mission was, we'd know where to look for him."

Hannah began pacing back and forth in front of the doctor's red brick office. She didn't know what to think. What had gotten into Mack? Splitting from Kerry and Lewis like that, making them all worry — after everything that had happened.

It was mean of Mack, that's what it was!

But Mack wasn't a mean person. He was smart and funny and kind.

Ah, but he was mean to Frog, a voice inside her head taunted.

"Hannah," Kerry said, "we have to get back to the station. Mack must already be back there."

"He couldn't have gone back without us seeing him," Hannah argued.

"Probably found a shortcut," Lewis said with one final glance up the street. There was no sign of Mack. "We can't wait here forever, or we'll have to hitchhike to California."

"I'm not leaving without Mack," Hannah said stubbornly.

Lewis was patient with her. "Let's just go back to the station and check, okay? If Mack's there, no problem. If he isn't, we'll tell the conductor and the detective and they'll hold the train until he shows up. And they'll help us look for him. We can't search this town by ourselves."

Hannah knew he was right. It would be stupid to separate and search for Mack in an unfamiliar city. If he wasn't at the station and they did have to look for him, they'd need help.

She nodded slowly, and they began walking. But she kept glancing back over her shoulder with anxious eyes. "He could be hurt," she murmured as they hurried along the street toward the station. "Something terrible could have happened to him." Like something terrible happened to Lolly and me, she added silently.

Lewis patted her shoulder sympathetically. "Listen, Hannah, if anyone can take care of himself, it's Mack. Quit worrying. He'll be at the station, I know he will."

But he wasn't.

The platform was crowded with noisy Parker High students, many of whom fell silent as she approached. Embarrassment washed over her. She hated everyone knowing how helpless she had been.

But she had more important worries now. Not one of the students staring at her was wearing a light blue shirt and a grin that curled her toes.

Dale was leaning against the railing opposite her. He was alone. She couldn't remember ever seeing him alone before. He'd always been with Frog or Lolly or Eugene, or, most often, all three.

Where was Eugene? Hadn't the two of them passed her only five or ten minutes ago? Maybe he'd stopped to buy gum or candy or mints in the terminal.

If only Mack had, too. But Lewis had checked, and there was no sign of Mack inside the building. Where *was* he?

Her face crumpled. "Oh, God, Lewis, he's not here!" she whispered, clutching at Lewis's sleeve. "He's not *here*!"

Frog's got him, came the voice in her head. Frog's got your precious Mack and it serves him right. Serves *you* right, too. You're as bad as he is.

"Don't panic," Lewis said, but his thin face was as anxious as Hannah's. "We'd better tell Ms. Quick. She'll freak, but she needs to know. And she'll have to tell the conductor to hold the train for Mack."

How long was a train allowed to wait before someone high up in the company gave the order to move it? she wondered.

"If Mack isn't on the train when it leaves," she announced, "I won't be, either."

"I heard Ms. Quick tell the conductor we weren't leaving without him, schedule or no schedule," Jean Marie said. "That should make you feel better."

Frog's got him, Frog's got him . . . the voice hissed in Hannah's ear. He's doing something terrible to your precious Mack while you stand around doing nothing. Some friend *you* are.

Hannah couldn't stand the thought of Mack in pain. She closed her eyes and leaned against the platform railing for support. Mack . . . .

"Here he comes!" Lewis cried jubilantly. "And he's okay, Hannah, look!"

Hannah's eyes flew open. They fastened on a red-faced, breathless Mack as he ran up the platform steps. His hair hung, wet with sweat, on his forehead, and his face was flushed with exertion. But he didn't look bruised or bloody.

Hannah was the first to cry, "Where have you *been*?" as she ran to him and dove into his chest, wrapping her grateful arms around him. "We thought something horrible had happened to you!"

"I got lost," he said quickly. "You okay? Did the doctor find anything wrong?"

"Never mind me, tell me where you *were*! You got *lost*?" Her relief was rapidly becoming overshadowed by annoyance. He had scared her half to death and now he didn't want to talk about it? Maybe — maybe because it was so awful, he *couldn't* talk about it? Or so bizarre that he was afraid no one would believe him?

"We were so worried," she said, backing away from Mack and waiting for his explanation. "Lewis said you yelled something and ran off. Why?"

Mack shrugged. "I feel like a fool — " he began.

But he was interrupted by Ms. Quick calling out to the conductor, who waited on the train steps, "Everyone present and accounted for!"

The conductor nodded and called, "All aboard!" adding, "C'mon, folks, we're behind schedule. Let's get a move on."

The crowd surged forward, taking Mack and Lewis with them and leaving Hannah behind with Kerry and Jean Marie.

"Mack!" Hannah cried, but he gave no sign that he'd heard her.

As the crowd propelled Hannah forward, she realized she hadn't accepted Mack's story about getting lost. Lost? When all he had to do was go straight up the street to the doctor's office? No way. He wasn't telling the truth, she was sure of it.

Why would Mack lie about where he'd been?

She had to know.

Taking a deep breath and extending her elbows on either side of her, Hannah pushed with all her might, creating a tiny space that allowed her to inch forward a little. She pushed again, and took another step. Mack and Lewis mounted the iron steps. She had to catch up to them.

"Hannah, wait up!" Kerry called from behind, but Hannah kept going. Mack and Lewis had their heads together, like two people sharing a secret. What Mack was saying was important, she knew it. And he didn't want her to hear, she knew that, too. Or he would have told her back at the station. He wouldn't have let himself get swept up by the crowd.

She tried to move closer, where she'd be able to overhear what he was telling Lewis. She was careful not to get too close — that was easy. All she had to do was mingle with the crowd heading from one car to the next. What wasn't so easy was inching her way toward Mack and Lewis. But she kept trying, and finally found herself separated from them by only one person, a small girl with a blonde ponytail.

Mack and Lewis didn't turn around.

By focusing her attention upon them, blocking out the rhythmic *clackety-clack* of the wheels, Hannah managed to make out what Mack was saying.

"Why are you arguing?" he asked Lewis, "I told you, I *know* it sounds crazy. But I could have sworn . . ."

The girl with the ponytail sneezed. Once. Twice. Three times.

Hannah felt like screaming. She had missed hearing whatever Mack could have sworn.

They entered a new car.

" . . . me get this straight," Lewis was saying. "We came out of the restaurant and started for the doctor's office to meet Hannah and you thought you saw . . . *what?*"

"Not what," Mack's voice replied clearly. "*Who.* I told you . . ." Hannah strained forward to hear.

"Someone was coming out of the drugstore on the corner. There was something about the way he walked, the way he moved, his hair . . . I would have sworn . . ."

Hannah held her breath. But she knew what Mack was going to say before he said it.

" . . . I would have sworn it was Frog."

Chapter 13

Hannah would have fallen to the floor if Mack hadn't heard her sharp intake of breath and turned to see her wavering in the aisle. He lunged for her, catching her before she could fall.

"You . . . saw . . . *Frog*?" she gasped, leaning into him.

"Oh, gosh, Hannah, no, you thought . . . geez, I'm sorry. I didn't know you were listening." Kerry and Jean Marie arrived in time to hear Mack add, "I *thought* it was him, but of course it wasn't."

"Who?" Kerry asked, seeing the look on Hannah's face. "Thought it was who?"

"*Frog*," Hannah breathed. "Mack saw Frog."

Kerry and Jean Marie gasped in unison even as Mack protested. "No! No, I didn't. How could I? This guy came out of the drugstore in town and he looked a lot like Frog. Dressed like him, too. Jeans and a plaid shirt with the sleeves rolled up, baseball cap. He looked so much like him, I lost my head and took off after him." Mack shook his head. "I don't know what I was thinking. I feel like a total jerk."

"But you're *not*!" Hannah cried. "It *was* him! I know he's alive, I can feel it. I didn't say anything because I knew you'd all think I was crazy, but now that Mack's *seen* him — "

"But I didn't!" Mack insisted. "That's just it. That's why I feel so foolish — "

"Did you catch up with the guy? Did you talk to him?" Hannah asked feverishly. "Did you *see* his face?"

Mack hesitated. "Well, no, but — "

"Then it *could* have been Frog! I knew it, I just knew it!"

"Hannah," Kerry warned, her eyes wide with bewilderment, "get a grip! What's wrong with you? Frog is dead. His coffin is right here on this train, remember?"

Hannah pounced. "Yes, but he's not *in* it! No one is. *I* ought to know. I was in there! So don't tell me Frog is dead. Someone else must have died in that car crash and Frog let everybody think it was him."

"Hannah," Jean Marie said softly, "that really doesn't make any sense. Why would Frog do that? If everyone thought he was dead, he'd never be able to show his face in town or at school, he couldn't go out or see people — why would someone do something so crazy?"

"That's just it," Hannah answered, her eyes glittering with fear, "he *is* crazy! Don't you get it? He faked his own death so he'd be free to get even with all of us for the nasty things we did to him. He knew that no matter what happened to any of us, no one would suspect him because everyone thinks he's dead. It's perfect." Her eyes traveled from one face to the next. "Can't you see that?"

Kerry shot a worried look at Mack. "But Hannah," she said, "*you're* the one who got locked in the coffin. And you're the only one who didn't have anything to confess in the Cafe. You're the only one who didn't do something terrible to Frog. So even if he is alive — and I don't think for one single second that he is — why would he hurt *you*?"

Hannah's cheeks blazed. "I have to get out of this awful hallway," she said quickly. "I can't breathe in here. Can we go back to our compartment, *please*? I'll feel safer there."

No one said anything as they all hurried back to the compartment, but Hannah knew what they were thinking. Their thoughts circled around her head like vultures about to descend: Hannah's losing it, Hannah's one slice of bread short of a loaf, Hannah thinks a dead guy is alive and walking this train. Poor Hannah!

Hannah bit down hard on her lower lip. She couldn't help how she felt, could she? *She* was the one who had been shut up in that horrible coffin, *she* was the one who knew better than anyone else that Frog wasn't in there. What was she supposed to think? That a dead person got out to make room for her?

That idea was even crazier than what *she* was thinking!

When they reached the compartment, she turned to face Mack. "So you ran after Frog," she said, biting off her words carefully. "That doesn't explain where you were all that time."

Mack's face flushed as he opened the compartment door and let them all step inside ahead of him. "I . . . I told you, I feel like a fool. What happened was, I ran after this . . . this person, whoever it was, and he went into a little wooden shed in one of the alleys. At least, I thought he did. But when I followed him inside, the place was empty. The door closed behind me and stuck. . . . I tried to get out and couldn't. The hinge was all rusty . . . guess the place hadn't been used much. Some kind of storage shed, I think. Anyway, I pounded and yelled and pushed, but nothing worked. I was stuck in there."

"Or *locked* in," Hannah said triumphantly. Her cheeks as flushed as Mack's, she turned to Kerry and said, "See? He was locked in that shed just like I was shut up inside the coffin. And I don't care what any of you say, it was *Frog* who did it!"

"No, Hannah," Mack protested, "no, it wasn't. I told you, the door was *stuck*, not locked. I got out by breaking a window and I went around to the front and checked the door. It wasn't locked."

"That doesn't mean it wasn't locked in the first

place," Hannah persisted. "He could have unlocked it after a while. And you never got close enough to get a good look at the person you were following, did you?"

"I didn't have to. I realized when I was in that shed that it was a crazy idea. We all know what happened to Frog."

"We all know what we *think* happened to Frog." Hannah, her arms folded against her chest, stood firm in the middle of the small, wood-panelled room. "Exactly what Frog *wanted* us to think."

Mack sighed heavily. "I give up. Think what you want to. Me, I'm going to check with that detective, see if he has any idea what's going on around here."

"Me, too," Lewis agreed. "I'll go with you."

When the compartment door had closed after them, Hannah turned to Kerry and Jean Marie and rolled her eyes heavenward. "They want me to admit that my theory is nuts," she said in exasperation, "and I just can't do that. I don't think it's nuts, do you?"

Their faces told her they thought exactly that.

Hannah's heart descended into her toes. She desperately wanted someone on her side.

Maybe it *was* a crazy theory. How could Frog fool the whole town into thinking he was dead? Didn't medical examiners check out things like that?

"Hannah," Kerry pointed out, "suppose, just suppose, you were right. Why would Frog hurt Lolly? She was the first one attacked, remember? But they were friends. More than friends. She was the only girl at school who would go out with him.

So why would he try to strangle her?"

"Well, I don't know about strangling, but they did have an awful fight," Jean Marie said.

Hannah stared at her. "They did? Frog and Lolly?"

"Well, she didn't call him Frog, Hannah. She called him Roger. Yeah, they did. Really nasty."

"How do you know?"

"I heard them. I mean, I wasn't eavesdropping, not on purpose. I was trying on jeans at The Gap, in the dressing room, and I heard these voices. I recognized Lolly's right away. She kept saying, 'You're not going, are you? Are you, Roger? You *can't* go!' "

Kerry looked interested. "Go where?"

Jean Marie shrugged. "How should I know?"

"What else did they say?" Hannah asked. Frog and Lolly had had a fight? She needed to know how *bad* the fight was.

"She kept saying he couldn't go, and he kept saying he was going. Then she said she was sure it was a joke and he was stupid not to see that and he screamed at her not to call him stupid, and then the clerk came over and threw them out. Told them to take their argument outside. The last thing I heard was Lolly saying something like, 'Then I'm going with you' and Frog saying 'You're not, you'll ruin everything.' Then she said, 'You're not going without me, Roger.' But their voices got too far away for me to hear the rest."

Hannah sank down onto one of the seats. Jean Marie had just answered for her the question of why

Frog would hurt Lolly. He'd been mad at her, maybe even as mad as he was at Hannah and her friends.

"When was this?" she asked quietly, her eyes on Jean Marie.

"Gosh, I don't remember, Hannah. I mean, why would I? It didn't matter to *me*." Jean Marie concentrated for a minute. "I think it was the Saturday before the trip. That morning."

Hannah exhaled deeply. She *knew* what Lolly and Frog had been fighting about.

That fight was *her* fault.

"Hannah," Kerry said, "quit looking so glum. A fight doesn't mean anything. I'm always arguing with boys and so far, not one of them has wrapped a noose around my neck."

"Not one of them was *Frog*," Hannah murmured stubbornly.

"Look, this is silly." Kerry grabbed her purse. "Come on, Jean Marie, let's leave Hannah here to rest — nobody needs rest more than Hannah does. I'll walk you back to your compartment. Then I'm going to take a shower."

"We're not supposed to go anywhere alone," Hannah reminded Kerry, alarm in her voice. "We promised Ms. Quick."

Kerry sighed in annoyance. "You're right. I forgot. Okay, then, Jean Marie needs a shower, too, don't you, Jean Marie?" Without waiting for an answer, she tugged at Jean Marie's sweater sleeve. "C'mon, we'll both take a shower. You rest, Hannah. I know you're nervous, so lock the door after us and, when we come back, I'll knock twice, then three times so you'll know it's me. Okay?"

Hannah nodded reluctantly.

Kerry collected her cosmetic case and towel, and then she and Jean Marie left the compartment.

Chapter 14

Hannah stood alone in the center of the small room, wishing briefly that she'd gone with them. But she was too worn-out to take a shower. Kerry was right: who needed rest more than Hannah Deaton?

She locked the door to the compartment. She would stay here, safe and sound, until Kerry and Jean Marie came back. She would rest, as promised.

The knock on the door as she was about to pull down the window shade wasn't Kerry's. No two-rap, three-rap deal, as Kerry had promised. It was an ordinary knock.

Backing away from the door, Hannah cried, "Who's there?"

"It's Ms. Quick, Hannah. I have the detective with me. He'd like to speak with you if you're feeling up to it."

Hannah let them in.

"I know it's hard to believe right now," Ms. Quick said, "but I actually have good news. I've received word that Lolly arrived home safely. Her parents were distraught, of course. Can't blame them. Now, if I can only get the rest of you to San Francisco intact. . . . Hannah, this is Detective Tesch. He has been assigned to help us. Please try to answer any questions he might have."

But, Hannah thought in silent protest, *I'm* the one with all the questions. Maybe this detective can give me some answers.

The man was short and balding and dressed in a neat brown suit and brown shirt, holding a round brown hat in his hands, which, Hannah noticed, were also brown: tanned and freckled. His brown shoes were shined to a high gloss. He didn't look anything like the detectives she'd seen on television.

As long as he could answer her questions, she didn't care *what* he looked like.

But he couldn't answer her questions. He was very nice, speaking softly and clearly, turning his brown hat around and around in his hands as he spoke, but he had no answers for her. He only had questions.

And Hannah had no answers. None that she could tell him. With Ms. Quick watching her with that frowny, worried look on her face, if Hannah told him what she was really thinking she knew she'd find herself off the train and in a padded cell before you could say, "Frog Drummond is alive and out for revenge."

The detective, whose name was Mr. Tesch, but whom Hannah had already named Mr. Brown, asked Hannah if she had seen the person who had imprisoned her in the "wooden box." He did *not* say "coffin." Maybe he thought it would upset her. He seemed like that sort of person.

When she told him no, she hadn't seen a thing, he nodded and asked her if she had any idea who it might have been. She had to bite her tongue.

"No," she lied. "I can't imagine . . ."

Her friends would have disagreed with that. They would have said the problem was, Hannah *could* imagine, and was doing just that.

But she *wasn't* — was she?

Mr. Brown-Tesch was no help. But he promised that he would check out the baggage car and "the . . . ah . . . place where you were held prisoner."

He made it sound like a jail, with bars and a sheriff and three meals a day. It hadn't been that nice.

"Why are you here alone?" Ms. Quick asked disapprovingly as they got up to leave.

"Kerry's taking a shower. It's okay. I'll keep the door locked. Where's Mack? Why isn't he with you?"

"He's talking to some of your classmates," the detective answered. "Helpful young man. Cares about you." He flushed slightly and shuffled his shiny brown shoes. "Grateful for the help. Don't you worry, miss, we'll find out how this happened. Could be a joke, maybe."

A sigh of disgust escaped from Hannah. He couldn't seriously think it was a joke, could he? Why did adults always think that bad things involving teenagers were just "jokes"? As if everyone Hannah knew was running around stuffing people into coffins, just for laughs.

She couldn't think of a single person who would think that was funny.

Well . . . scratch that. Maybe *one* person.

The two adults left, both visibly disappointed that Hannah hadn't had any answers. Ms. Quick warned her to stay in her compartment until her friends returned, and the detective asked her to "keep thinking. You might remember something that you've forgotten because you've been upset."

She closed the door after them, feeling more frustrated than when they'd arrived. She had expected so much help from the detective. But he, like everyone else, believed that Frog was dead. So how could the detective help her?

How could anyone?

Despondent, she stood looking out the window at the passing landscape for a few minutes before deciding she wasn't accomplishing anything. Better to rest as she'd promised. She'd be able to think more clearly when her mind was fresh.

It was too bright in the room for sleep. Hannah pulled the shades, plunging the room into an artificial "night." In the train station she and Kerry had tossed a coin to decide who got the upper berth. Kerry had lost. The climb up the little ladder was hers.

But I would feel safer up there, Hannah thought decisively, and moved to open the latch that held the upper bunk flat against the wall when not in use.

It seemed wrong, somehow, to be wasting time on sleep during her "educational excursion." But so far, the only education she'd received was the knowledge that someone was out to get her. She might not be learning any geography while she was napping, but at least she'd be *safe.*

The bunk, already made-up, fell forward, and Hannah clambered up the ladder and onto the bed.

Her knee hit something. She couldn't see, but she knew there was a small reading light up there. Her hand reached out, her fingers searching the wall for the switch.

As her fingers fumbled along the panelling, she noticed a sharp, oddly unpleasant odor. In the darkness, she tried to make out the shape of the long, bulky object on the bed. Had Kerry sneaked in a garment bag full of clothes and stashed it up here, figuring she'd move it before they went to bed that night? It seemed like the kind of thing Kerry would do. At last Hannah's fingers found the light switch. She turned it on.

It wasn't much of a light. The little bulb provided only a faint, sickly glow.

But, faint though it was, the glow illuminated the thing in Kerry's bunk.

And it wasn't a garment bag.

Hannah's mouth dropped open, but no sound emerged. Her eyes fastened in horror on the disgusting thing lying there on its back, stiff and unforgiving, emanating a strange odor. The eyes stared, unseeing, up toward the ceiling and the face was raw and ruined — a face she had once known —

a face almost unrecognizable because of the blazing inferno that had tortured it, and nearly consumed it. . . .

She had been right, after all.

Frog Drummond was not in his coffin where he belonged.

Frog Drummond was in Kerry's bunk.

Chapter 15

Voiceless with horror, Hannah toppled backward off the berth. When she hit the floor, she scuttled, crablike, until her back smacked up against the seat opposite the bunks. Eyes and mouth wide open in shock, she crouched there, silent and trembling.

Minutes passed. Hannah sat frozen, her eyes rivetted on the upper berth, her fisted hands pressed against her mouth.

Then she began shaking her head from side to side. The sound she uttered was a muted grunt of denial that, once started, she couldn't stop. "Uhuh-uhuh," she moaned, head swinging from side to side, eyes dull with shock. "Uhuhuhuh."

But the dull glaze in her eyes quickly changed to bright, blazing terror.

She had to get out of there. Away from . . . *it.*

When she finally moved, she was no longer making a sound. She had sealed her lips, as if staying really, really quiet, might keep the thing on her bunk from coming after her. She crawled, sideways, still staring at the upper berth, until she was at the door. Reaching up, she unlatched it and yanked it open. Still mute, she threw herself out into the hall.

The door swung shut behind her.

For several seconds, Hannah lay on the dark carpet in the empty corridor, now allowing herself an anguished moan.

But the room right behind her held such horror, she couldn't stay there. She had to move, to escape, to seek safety. Away from that . . . that *thing*.

Scrambling to her feet, Hannah stumbled down the aisle. She still didn't scream. She was afraid to. It . . . might hear her.

She had half-run half-stumbled all the way to the end of the car when she realized she was headed in the wrong direction. Both Mack and Lewis's compartment and the showers were at the opposite end of the car.

Hannah groaned in dismay. She sagged against the wall. Why didn't someone come to help her? Where *was* everyone?

She couldn't stay here. Turning, she reversed her steps.

But when she reached a point of several feet beyond her compartment, she found that she couldn't continue. Her feet came to a complete halt on the carpet and refused to move.

"Help me," Hannah whispered, and began weeping.

She was still standing there, still weeping in despair when Kerry, in her white terrycloth robe, and Jean Marie, in her hot pink robe, emerged from the showers and saw her.

Kerry waved, Jean Marie called out something friendly, and Hannah watched through a haze of tears. They don't know, she thought dully. They don't know that I'm paralyzed here and they don't know what's waiting for them in the compartment. I can't tell them. I can't!

But she knew she would have to.

"Hannah?" Jean Marie asked as they approached and realized she wasn't directly outside the compartment as they had first thought. "What are you doing?"

"You're crying," Kerry said, hurrying over to Hannah. "What's wrong? I thought you were taking a nap." Alarm slid into her voice. "Hannah? *What?*"

"I . . . I . . ." Hannah swallowed hard. "Frog . . ."

"Get someone!" Kerry ordered Jean Marie. "Hurry!"

Jean Marie ran.

All Hannah could do was point toward the compartment with a shaky finger.

"I don't know why you're such a mess," Kerry said, putting an arm around Hannah's shoulders, "but from the look on your face, I'm guessing we won't go back into the compartment until Jean Marie gets here with help." With an edge of the wet towel hanging over her arm she swiped gently at Hannah's tear-streaked face. "Okay, Hannah?" Kerry asked softly, patting Hannah's shoulder.

"We'll just wait right here in the hall for Jean Marie."

Gulping gratefully, Hannah nodded in relief.

A few minutes later, Jean Marie ran down the corridor, followed by Mack and Lewis.

"Where *were* you guys?" Kerry demanded. "Something's happened. Why didn't you hear anything?"

"Playing pool," Mack answered. "In the rec center. Everybody's up there. What's going on?" His eyes went to Hannah's face. "I thought you were sleeping or I'd have been here. What happened?"

Alerted by the commotion, the conductor and Ms. Quick arrived.

All Hannah could say was, "In there," pointing to the compartment, "in the upper berth."

Kerry swallowed her curiosity and stayed with Hannah while the others opened the door and went inside.

They were only in there a few minutes. When they emerged, every face registered bewilderment.

"What?" Mack asked Hannah again. "We didn't see anything. What are we looking for?"

"In . . . in the upper *berth*," she managed. "I told you, in the upper berth."

Mack nodded. "Yeah. We looked. Nothing there."

Hannah blanched. "What? No, no, that's not right. Look again, Mack, please! There's . . . there's something there, there *is*! I *saw* it . . . I felt it . . ." her voice fell to a murmur.

His mouth grim, Mack turned and went back

inside the compartment. Ms. Quick and the conductor looked at Hannah, and then at each other, but no one said anything.

When Mack came back out, he was shaking his head. "There isn't anything there, Hannah, honest. I looked. I can tell someone was sleeping there, because the sheets are all messed up. But that's it. Come see for yourself."

"No!" Hannah shrieked, recoiling. "No! I'm not going back in there. Frog was there, he was! He was in my bunk just lying there, staring up at the ceiling and his face . . ." She sobbed, and her hands went to her mouth . . . "His face . . . it was horrible . . . all burned . . ."

"Hannah, stop this right now!" Ms. Quick said sharply, coming over to put an arm around her. "You fell asleep, you had a nightmare . . . understandable considering what you've been through. But you're going to make yourself sick. You must calm down."

Hannah lifted her head. "A dream?" she cried. "A dream? I hadn't even," she bit off the words, "*gone to sleep*!" She looked from one person to the next. "How could I? I couldn't climb onto the berth because he . . . he was in the way! So how could I have gone to sleep?"

Ms. Quick patted her shoulder. "Many times in nightmares we believe that we were awake the whole time. You must know that, Hannah. I'm sure this isn't the first bad dream you've ever had."

"It wasn't a dream!" Hannah shrieked. "I keep telling you — " But she could see no one believed her. Pulling free of Kerry's arm and Ms. Quick's hand, Hannah shouted, "I'll *show* you! I'll go back in there if that's the only way I can prove . . ." Taking a deep breath, she ran to the compartment, yanked the door open and burst inside crying out, "Come! Come and look and you'll see!"

Her heart was thudding sickeningly, her breathing labored as she stopped short directly opposite the upper berth, still suspended like a roof over her own, exactly as she had left it.

No, *not* exactly.

Except for rumpled white sheets, the bunk was empty.

Chapter 16

Hannah stared, disbelieving, at the empty berth.

"But I . . ." she whispered. "I . . ."

"It's okay, Hannah," Kerry said quickly, pushing Lewis and Mack aside to wrap an arm around Hannah's shoulders, "you just had a really rotten dream, that's all. Because of last night, I'll bet. I mean, you couldn't be over that horrible business already. I'd have nightmares, too, if I were you. We shouldn't have left you here alone."

Mack nodded agreement. "I can't believe we were playing pool and having a high old time while you were wrestling with demons. I'm sorry, Hannah."

"Me, too," Lewis said solemnly. "We'll stick together from now on, I promise."

Unable to speak, Hannah stared silently at the berth. I wasn't even asleep yet. I was still awake when I saw . . . that *thing*.

But there was nothing there. How could she argue with that? She saw it, they all saw it: the empty berth, with the sheets rumpled, as if someone had been sleeping in it. That someone had been her.

A dream? It had been a dream — a nightmare? She hadn't really seen it?

A long, deep shudder escaped from Hannah. She *had* seen it. Let them think what they wanted. She knew what she'd seen with her own eyes. But if she kept arguing, if she insisted that she had seen a dead person in her bunk, everyone would think the train had taken her into the *Twilight Zone* for good.

But, the thing was, it hadn't *been* a dead body. She knew that now. At first, when she'd seen it, of course she'd thought it was dead. Oh, it was burned, all right — horribly. But it had to be alive. How else would it have gotten up into the upper berth, and then gotten away. It was just *pretending* to be dead, to scare her. And scare her it had. No wonder there had been room for her in Frog's coffin. *He* wasn't using it. *He* was roaming around the train, hurting people and trying to scare them to death. Now Hannah knew for sure that Frog was alive and on the train. She had *seen* him.

She should have left the train when Lolly did. By the time they arrived in San Francisco, if they ever did, the last shred of her sanity would be gone like the landscape that whizzed by as the train raced across the tracks.

"I can't get through this day." Her voice was solemn and soft. "I can't. I don't want to be on this train anymore."

Everyone started talking at once, reassuring her, telling her they would stay with her and keep her safe. Mack said he wouldn't leave her side,

Lewis nodded agreement, Kerry held her hand and Ms. Quick thrust two aspirin and a paper cup full of water in Hannah's face.

None of it helped. How could they keep her safe from Frog when none of them believed he was after her? She wasn't going to bring it up again. She couldn't bear the looks that would appear on their faces. She would just do what they had told her to, go where they wanted her to, say what she thought they wanted to hear — but stay alert and on guard every single second, watching for him . . . waiting.

Sooner or later, he'd show up.

"You should sleep," Mack said. "You look really beat."

Hannah lifted her head. She wiped her face free of tears with the tissue Kerry had given her, tossed her head to shake her hair in place, and stood up. "I can't sleep. Let's do something. You said everyone was at the rec center. Let's go there."

Mack frowned. "You sure? Look, I'll stay here while you sleep."

"No. I don't want to sleep." She tried to smile brightly at the cluster of people gathered around her in the compartment. "You guys were right. It was just a bad dream. But I don't want to have it again. So let's play. That's what we're here for, right?"

Kerry looked at her with a quizzical expression on her face and said, "Well, if you're sure that's what you want, they're showing a movie this afternoon. We could grab some lunch in the Cafe and then watch Schwarzenegger get the bad guys."

"Sounds great!" Hannah said. "Let's go!"

The relief that appeared on every face told her she was doing the right thing, although Mack still looked uncertain. She could practically hear them thinking, Oh, good, everything's okay now. Everything's back to normal.

She would keep to herself the belief that absolutely *nothing* was normal. "Well, let's go!" she repeated, and led the way out of the compartment.

When they entered the recreation area where the movie was being shown, everyone seemed to be having a good time. Except for Dale and Eugene, who sat together off to Hannah's left staring stonily at the blank screen, everyone had apparently suspended all thoughts of danger. They cheered happily when the room went dark and the screen lit up.

Hannah didn't cheer. Sitting in a pitch-black, crowded room watching bodies being blown into oblivion was not what she needed. By concentrating with all of her might, she was able to tune out the on-screen mayhem and listen for a sound out of the ordinary, a movement that might be threatening, any sign that danger could be approaching in the total darkness.

That sound, when it came, wasn't the scream or shriek of pain that she was expecting. It was a sharp, *whizzing* sound that sent Hannah's head into an instinctive ducking motion. It came during the last few seconds of the film and no one around her seemed to notice the sound or the startled "Uh!" that followed. Afterward, Hannah would remember thinking at that exact moment, There! There it is! Something bad has happened.

And, following that thought came another: He's here. Frog is here.

She sat perfectly still, waiting, as the movie ended and people around her clapped and shouted their approval. The credits rolled, the lights came on, and she didn't move. Her eyes blinked steadily, but she was waiting.

People stood up, stretched, yawned, grinned at each other.

Mack stood up. Kerry and Jean Marie stood up.

Lewis did not stand up. He remained sitting in his chair.

And he said, slowly and with awe in his voice, "I think I've been stabbed." Hannah's silent reaction was, Well, of course you have. That sound I heard was the knife whizzing through the air. Then I heard you cry out. And I know Frog is here, so I'm not the least bit surprised.

Outwardly, she did what everyone else did. She hurried to Lewis's side in alarm.

The weapon wasn't a knife, after all. It was an ice pick. The thick wooden handle protruded from the back of Lewis's leather theater seat, while the sharp, narrow pick itself had penetrated the seat and impaled the flesh near Lewis's collarbone. A small but vivid red stain etched a half-moon, like some trendy trademark, on his white sweater. The half-moon was slowly oozing into a three-quarter moon, and Lewis's face was the murky beige of swamp water.

"Oh, my God," Kerry breathed.

"I don't think it's that bad," Mack hastened to reassure her. He knelt beside Lewis. "Too high. Hit the bone, I think." The crowd moving up the aisle past them, preoccupied with discussing the movie, seemed unaware of anything unusual until Mack called out, "Someone get the conductor! And Mr. Dobbs or Ms. Quick. Hurry up!"

Kerry lifted a pale face to Hannah and said angrily, "I *knew* we'd need that doctor! And now he's not here, all because of Lolly!"

But it wasn't Lolly's fault she almost got strangled, Hannah thought, and wondered if now someone would believe that Frog was alive and on the train.

Not that it mattered. She had already made up her mind. She was going to make sure, once and for all, that she was right.

There was only one way to do that.

She was going to open Frog's coffin.

Chapter 17

The fact that Lewis's wound proved to be minor, speedily disinfected and bandaged by Ms. Quick, failed to change Hannah's mind about making a trip to the baggage car.

And the fact that the detective had no answers for them, except to say that the ice pick had been stolen from the dining car, only intensified her determination to see for herself whether or not Frog was in his proper place.

If I don't, she thought as they all accompanied a shaken Lewis back to his compartment, I will *not* make it through the rest of this trip. One way or the other, I have to know.

She didn't want to tell anyone what she was planning. Their response, she was positive, would be disheartening. But there was no way on earth she was going into that baggage car alone.

They all went back to Lewis and Mack's compartment.

Hannah waited until the color had returned to Lewis's face. Then she announced firmly, "I'm going to the baggage car after dinner. I want to see for myself that Frog really is dead and he's where he belongs."

Lewis, Kerry, and Jean Marie gasped. But Mack only nodded. "I knew that's what you were thinking," he said. "I saw the look on your face when you spotted the ice pick in Lewis. You're going to open the coffin?"

Hannah nodded. "I have to." She knew that had Mack not been on her side, she wouldn't have had a chance of talking the others into joining her. She reached out and touched his arm in gratitude. "I have to know."

Kerry was still aghast. "Hannah, you *know* it's going to be horrible! He *burned* to death, for pete's sake!"

Hannah opened the door. "You're forgetting, Kerry, I've already *seen* him. Nightmare or not, what I saw in that upper berth is what Frog would look like now. So it won't be a complete shock to me. Are you coming with me?"

"I am," Lewis said, getting to his feet. He didn't waver, and seemed his old self. "I want to know who thinks I'd make a great ice cube."

"If Lewis can go when he's been hurt," Jean Marie said, "I'm not going to chicken out. I'm with you, Hannah."

"Well, I'm certainly not going to wait alone somewhere for you guys," Kerry exclaimed. "I think the whole idea is totally repulsive and useless. Frog is dead as a doornail and isn't bothering anyone. But if you have to, Hannah, you have to. So I'm going, too." But she added grimly as she stood up, "Just don't expect me to look, that's all. I'd die first!"

If we *don't* look, Hannah thought as they left for the dining car, you might die anyway, Kerry. Lolly almost did and I could have suffocated in that coffin, and an inch or two lower with that ice pick would have left you with no boyfriend. Whether Kerry thought so or not, they were doing the right thing.

They told no one of their plans.

Everyone at dinner was glad to see that Lewis was okay. To Hannah's surprise, Dale and Eugene stopped him at the entrance and asked how he was feeling. Lewis was as surprised as Hannah. "Fine," he mumbled.

"You were lucky," Dale said, moving away. "An inch or two lower or higher and . . ."

Eugene raised a hand to make a slicing motion across his own throat. "Yeah, you'd be up in heaven right now with good old Frog," he said with a grin. Then the two left to take a table at the rear of the car.

"Those two are weird," Lewis murmured. "In heaven? Aren't they awfully optimistic about Frog's final destination?"

"They're assuming an awful lot just by believing that he's *dead*," Hannah said sharply. "We won't know that for sure until we check that coffin."

There was a lot of complaining among the students about the detective asking too many questions and getting too few results.

"Some fun trip," one girl groused loudly. "I was just about to take a nice, long shower when he showed up at my door, asking me if I'd seen or heard anything unusual. Is he kidding? This whole *trip* is nuts!"

Another girl at the same table nodded in agreement. "I'm afraid to step outside our compartment alone. At first I thought what happened to that girl in the Cafe was somebody's idea of a sick joke. But what happened to Lewis sure wasn't funny."

Everyone agreed that it wasn't the least bit funny.

There was no laughter or light chatter in the dining car that night. Hannah couldn't help thinking how different the atmosphere was from the way it had been in the Cafe that first morning — before the attack on Lolly. She knew why they were all afraid.

Because there was no place to run to on a train.

After dinner, they gathered in Mack and Lewis's compartment, which was closest to the baggage car, until their fellow passengers had taken refuge in their own secure little rooms.

"We have to be quiet," Hannah warned, opening the door and peering out. "Ms. Quick is a nervous wreck. The slightest sound will set her off and she'll be hot on our trail. And that detective is still roaming around, too. Everyone tiptoe, okay?"

They had no flashlight. The corridors were dimly lit but the baggage car would be dark. As they made their way down the corridor, Lewis pointed out in a whisper that if they turned on a light, someone might see it from under the door.

"No one's going to be around," Hannah argued. "Not at this time of the night. Everyone's hiding in their compartments. But we probably shouldn't take any chances. We'll leave the light off."

"Someone should keep an eye out for the conductor," Jean Marie suggested. "I'll do it if you want. I'll wait outside and if I see him coming, I'll knock twice."

"No way," Lewis protested. "No one's doing anything alone. We go in together and take our chances together, period."

"If we get caught," Kerry said, "we'll make up some story. I'll say I needed something from my bag."

"Right," Lewis whispered in agreement. "Nobody will have trouble believing that."

The cars through which they passed were so still, so silent. No happy chatter, no giggling or laughter, no cheerful music sounded from behind closed doors. Only an occasional, nervous murmuring competed with the steady *ga-dink* of the wheels on the tracks.

Slowly, carefully, Mack pulled the baggage car door open. He checked to make sure no porter or conductor was around and then gestured that it was safe to enter.

"Can't see a thing," he murmured. They fell all over each other in the dark, a jumbled mass of confusion, all colliding elbows and knees and shoulders as they tried to get their bearings.

Then they moved off, cautiously, into the thick curtain of darkness.

"I don't need to see," Hannah whispered. "I can find the coffin in the dark. I know exactly where it is."

"How are you going to know if he's *in* there when you can't see?" Kerry asked.

Hannah began to move forward carefully, feeling with her feet for piles of luggage or boxes. "I'll know. I'll know the minute I open it."

"Then I'm *glad* it's so dark in here," Kerry said. "This way, you won't be able to see his face." To Lewis she said, "Under no circumstances let go of my hand. If you do, I'll scream."

With Mack holding her hand, and Lewis and Kerry and Jean Marie holding on to one another, Hannah slowly, carefully led the way across the baggage car to where the coffin was. As her eyes became accustomed to the gloom, she could make out shapes and was able to avoid several piles of luggage and stacks of boxes. Lewis tripped once and uttered a mild oath, and Kerry, following closely behind him, bumped into him and nearly fell.

Hannah knew that under any other circumstances, they all would have been laughing hysterically. But not now. Not in here.

"I don't see why we can't turn on the light," Kerry complained. "You said yourself, Hannah, there's no one out there now. I'm going to trip and break my neck."

Hannah shook her head. "No. I don't want a light on. Because when I lift the lid, if Frog's in there, you'll see him and scream your head off. Everyone on the train will come running. Just watch where you're going."

"How can I watch where I'm going when I can't *see*?" But Kerry subsided then, and they continued picking their slow, careful, silent way through the darkness.

Determined though Hannah was, she was shaking by the time they reached the long, solid shape sitting at chest-level against the wall. For one blank second, she couldn't remember why she was there.

Then she reminded herself, I am doing this so that I will know if Frog is the one who's been terrorizing us.

Hannah turned to peer into the blackness shrouding her friends. "Ready?" she whispered.

"No," Kerry said, "but you're going to open it anyway, so go ahead."

Mack whispered, "Ready? I'll help. You can't lift that lid by yourself." And he moved forward to grip the edge of the lid.

"On the count of three," Hannah said, her pulse racing wildly. "One . . . two . . . three . . ."

They had lifted the lid less than an inch when the click of a switch broke the breathless silence and the overhead light went on.

Blinking in surprise the five whirled simultaneously, as if they were attached.

The conductor stood in the doorway.

"What in blazes do you think you're doing?"

Chapter 18

Hannah flushed guiltily as all four hands instinctively let go of the lid, and it thudded shut. Hannah knew that no excuse in the world would convince the conductor that what they'd been about to do was the right thing. The truth, in this case, wasn't going to do the trick. She'd have to come up with something better.

The angry conductor began striding across the room toward them.

"I asked what you thought you were doing," the conductor demanded. "Am I crazy or were you people about to open that coffin?"

It sounded to Hannah as if he wasn't sure exactly what he had seen. Probably because he couldn't believe what his own eyes had told him. Too gross, even for teenagers.

"We were just looking for something," she said quickly, taking a half step forward. "I'm the one who was shut in the coffin, remember?"

He nodded slowly, suspicion still clouding his eyes.

"Well, I lost a very valuable ring, one my grandmother gave me, and I've looked everywhere else. So I decided it must have come off in here somewhere. My friends offered to help me look."

"You weren't trying to open that coffin?" he asked. It was clear he wanted to believe her, but was still unsure.

Hannah gasped. "*Open* it? You really think after what happened to me, I'd open that thing?" There, she hadn't actually lied. She had simply asked a question.

The conductor looked dubious. "Looked to me like the three of you had your hands on the coffin."

"We were checking the edges to see if maybe it was somewhere around here. But," Hannah said with feigned disappointment, "it's not."

"I don't want you kids messing around in here," the conductor said sternly. "Can't have that."

Hannah's cold bones warmed with relief. He'd bought her story.

"Didn't your teacher tell you to stay in your compartments?" he added, disapproval heavy in the words.

Hannah nodded contritely, her eyes on the floor. "Yes, sir, she did. And that's where we're going, right this minute, I promise. Thanks for being a good guy."

He *harumphed* and stood aside to let them pass.

Flashing him grateful smiles, they all hurried out of the baggage car.

But the smiles quickly faded as they exited into the dim, empty corridor.

"Well, that certainly was a waste of time!" Kerry announced in disgust. "You guys hardly even got the lid open. We almost got into serious trouble, and for nothing!"

"It wasn't for nothing," Hannah said calmly, "and it wasn't a waste of time." She moved ahead to lead the way back. "I found out what I wanted to know."

Chapter 19

Kerry stopped in her tracks. "You couldn't have!" she cried. "How could you have found out anything? That lid wasn't open more than a crack."

Hannah turned to face her friends. "That was enough. Frog was in there." She could hardly believe it herself, but it was true. She had seen it with her own eyes. Still, where had he been while *she* was in there?

Jean Marie moved forward. "How could you tell, Hannah? I agree with Kerry. The conductor turned on the light too soon."

"No. No, he didn't. I saw that tattoo."

Mack frowned. "Tattoo? What tattoo?"

Hannah leaned against the paisleyed wall. "Frog had a tattoo on his left wrist. It was gross. A rat with wings and bared fangs." She shuddered. "It was ugly. And that's what I saw in the coffin. A wrist with a winged rat tattooed on it. Nobody else at school had anything like that. So I knew it was Frog." She shook her head in disbelief. "I was so sure . . ."

"Well, you were the only one who thought he might not be in there," Kerry pointed out. Relief filled her voice as she added, "I'm glad that's over!"

Hannah lifted her head. "Kerry, aren't you forgetting something? All we know now is that Frog really is dead and where he's supposed to be. But that doesn't explain anything else. We still don't know who hurt Lolly and put me in the coffin and stabbed Lewis. Or, for that matter, where Frog's body was when I was in there."

The door to the baggage car opened and the conductor stuck his head out to deliver a stern glare.

"C'mon, let's go," Lewis urged. "We can think better back in one of the compartments. We'll talk about it there."

Hannah insisted they stop at Lewis and Mack's compartment. "I'm not going back into ours," she said firmly. "I couldn't sleep in that bunk no matter how beat I was. Not after this morning."

Kerry groaned. "Oh, Hannah, I thought you agreed that was just a terrible nightmare. Are you telling me we're not going to get a good night's sleep tonight? After the day we've had? I'm not sleeping in that compartment alone! And at least you know now that Frog couldn't possibly have been in your bed, right?"

Hannah didn't answer until they were safely inside and seated, with the door locked. "Kerry," she said slowly, deliberately, "Frog may be where he belongs, but there's someone *else* out to get us. And whoever it is *knows* which compartment is ours." She glanced at the faces of the other three. "I don't think *any* of us should stay in our compartments tonight. It's not safe."

While they pondered that, Hannah stared out the window, filled now with their pale reflections and, beyond those images, the soft golden haze of distant lights. I wish I were there, Hannah thought. I wish I were in that town, in one of those houses or one of those cars on the highway. I'd be safe there.

She couldn't stop thinking about Frog. Okay, he was in the coffin now, where he belonged.

But where had he been while *she* was in there? And how had he appeared in Kerry's bunk that afternoon? The thought that someone might have taken him out, removed his body and placed it elsewhere, was sickening. How could anyone do something so horrible?

Still, was moving a body any more horrible than strangling someone or trying to suffocate someone in a closed box or splintering someone's flesh with an ice pick? Someone who would do one of those things probably wouldn't even hesitate to lift a corpse from its place of rest and deposit it elsewhere.

"I have an idea," Mack said, leaning forward on the seat. "Why don't we go to the Observation Lounge? Nobody will be there this time of night. We won't be able to see anything out of all that glass, but we'll have it to ourselves. No one will expect us to be up there, so we should be safe, right?"

"Is it open?" Lewis asked.

"I think it's always open. Worth a try, right?"

The idea appealed to Hannah. Simply being somewhere unexpected would give them an edge. No one would think to look for them up in the Observation Lounge.

"I'm for it," she said eagerly. "Jean Marie?"

Jean Marie nodded. "But I'll have to go tell my roomies I'm staying with you guys tonight, or they'll call out the guards. I won't say where we're staying, though. Come with me?"

They all went together, first to Jean Marie's compartment, where one of her roommates questioned her three times before finally opening the compartment door less than an inch to peer out. Then they went on to the Observation Lounge.

It was open. And empty.

"Told you," Mack said in obvious relief. The car, decorated all in blue, seemed larger than any of the others because of the wide expanse of glass on ceiling and walls. There were comfortable seats to lounge on and tables and chairs stationed in windowed corners.

"I wish we had something to eat," Lewis said as he took a seat and pulled Kerry down beside him. "I'm starving!"

"They'd feed you here during the day," Hannah said. She and Mack took the seat opposite Kerry and Lewis, while Jean Marie grabbed a seat for herself across the aisle. "Snacks and Cokes. But not now. Too late."

"I could get something to eat in Salt Lake City. We stop there in half an hour."

"Ms. Quick will never let you off the train," Jean

Marie said, curling up in a little ball with her head on the armrest. "No one's supposed to get off. I heard her tell the conductor."

"No one's going to feed you, Lewis," Kerry said, "so you might as well go to sleep."

Hannah had already closed her eyes. She leaned her head against Mack's shoulder and tried to close off her mind as well.

But it wouldn't stop churning. Were they really safe here? Maybe someone had heard them sneaking through the cars for a second time that night. Maybe whoever was after them would check the compartments, find them empty, and begin searching the entire train. Sooner or later, their stalker, whoever it was, would arrive at this car.

I won't sleep, she resolved, I'll stay awake all night. It's the only way to be sure.

But Mack's chest felt safe and solid and she was exhausted . . .

Chapter 20

When Hannah next opened her eyes, it was morning. The others awakened, too, stretching and groaning, to bright desert sunshine blazing down upon them as the train sped across Nevada.

"I feel like I slept in a sandbox," Jean Marie moaned. "I'm all itchy."

"My neck hurts," Kerry complained, and the first words out of Lewis's mouth were, "I'm starving."

But all Hannah could think was, We're all safe. We're all still here and we're safe.

She smiled sleepily at Mack. "You were right about coming here," she said softly. "It was a super idea. Did you sleep?"

He nodded and rubbed the back of his neck. "Yeah. I wasn't going to, but when no one showed up by three in the morning, I guess I relaxed and fell asleep. Not much of a protector, am I?"

"I think you must be," she disagreed, "because here we all are, and we're all in one piece."

"*Five* pieces," Lewis corrected. His curly hair was askew, with little carroty bunches sticking out every which way and he moved stiffly, the result of sleeping sitting up with Kerry's head on his chest. "Now, can we please go eat before I shrivel up and die right here on the spot?"

"I have to take a shower first," Jean Marie announced, standing up and stretching. "I cannot possibly go into the dining car or the Cafe looking like I slept under the train instead of in it. But I'll hurry, Lewis, I promise."

Lewis made a face, but when Kerry and Hannah both agreed that a shower had to precede breakfast, he gave in and agreed to wait for them.

"We'll stand guard," he volunteered, "me and Mack. But we're only giving you five minutes, not a second more, understood?"

What they understood even as they nodded agreement was that Kerry Oliver had never taken a shower and dressed in less than thirty minutes in her entire life. But they also understood that Mack and Lewis would wait outside the shower room for them no matter how long it took.

The girls gathered their shower things and fresh clothing from their compartments.

"You are the only redhead I know who would dare wear that horrible shade of pink," Kerry teased Jean Marie as they hurried to the shower room, robes over their arms.

Jean Marie laughed. "It's just a robe, Kerry. I'm not planning to wear it in public."

"Quit arguing," Hannah said mildly. "If we don't hurry up, the showers will be filled to overflowing with bodies."

But the white tiled room was empty when they arrived. Hannah felt safe with Mack and Lewis stationed outside, and after a night's sleep, restless though it may have been, she felt more optimistic than she had since the attack on Lolly. Frog was where he belonged and as far as they knew, there had been no new attacks during the night. There had been no screaming, no uproar, no commotion — maybe it was all over now. Maybe their crazy tormentor had been scared off by the appearance of the railroad detective and had left the train in Salt Lake City last night.

Comforted by that thought, Hannah stepped inside one of the three shower cubicles. Kerry and Jean Marie did the same.

Jean Marie finished first. Over the roar of rushing water, Hannah heard a shower door close and knew it was Jean Marie's. Kerry had that mane of long black hair to wash and rinse. She couldn't possibly be done already.

Lathering her own hair with shampoo, Hannah thought, Jean Marie and I will both be dressed and ready to go long before Kerry, and then we'll have to be patient while she fools with that hair of hers. Mack and Lewis will go nuts, waiting.

But the aches and pains of an awkward sleeping position disappeared under the soothing hot water. It felt so good, Hannah hated to turn it off. She stayed in the shower longer than usual.

Finally, the thought of Mack and Lewis waiting stabbed her with guilt. Sighing, she turned off the water. Kerry's shower was still going strong.

Hannah fumbled for her towel.

It wasn't hanging on the door where she thought she'd put it.

"Hey, Jean Marie," she called, swiping at the water running down her cheeks, "grab my towel, will you? I think I left it on that little bench over there."

There was no answer. How could anyone hear anything over the thundering rush of Kerry's shower water?

Hannah raised her voice. "Jean Marie? Are you out there?"

Nothing.

She must have already left to join Lewis and Mack. How could someone who always looked so together dress that quickly?

Mumbling under her breath, Hannah left the cubicle and found her towel and her clothes. Drying and dressing quickly, turbanning her hair in the damp towel, she yelled at Kerry to "get a move on" and pulled the door open.

Mack and Lewis were talking to Eugene. When they spotted Hannah, they moved forward eagerly. Eugene left abruptly, as if he was trying to avoid Hannah.

"Finally!" Lewis exclaimed, "now we can go eat." He patted his stomach. "Where's Kerry?"

"Still in the shower." Hannah's eyes surveyed the corridor. "Where'd Jean Marie go?"

Mack and Lewis exchanged confused glances. Mack spoke first. "Jean Marie? She didn't go anywhere. We haven't seen her."

Hannah tilted her head. "Very funny. Now, where is she? If she's hiding and it was your idea, your sense of humor is sick. It's not funny."

Mack took a step forward. "Hannah, Jean Marie didn't come out here. She must still be in the shower."

Hannah jolted upright and sucked in her breath. "You're not kidding, are you? She really didn't come out here?"

He shook his head. Lewis did the same.

"But . . . but she's not in here with us." Hannah glanced over her shoulder, into the shower room. "She's *not.* And there's . . . there's no place to hide in here. My cubicle and Jean Marie's are empty and Kerry's still in hers."

"Hannah!" Kerry shrieked, "do you have the door open? I can feel cold air. Cut it out!"

"Wait a sec," Hannah told the boys, closing the shower room door. "Jean Marie?" she called, although it was quite clear there was no place to hide in the tiny room. It held no secret niches, no roomy nooks and crannies. Besides the three skinny cubicles, there was only a small white bench sitting in the middle of the room.

When Hannah said the name again, her voice came out in little more than a tremulous whisper. "Jean Marie?"

There was no answer.

There was only the constant drumming of a steady stream of water pulsating from Kerry's shower head.

Chapter 21

A crowd gathered in the corridor outside the shower room as the railroad detective checked things out. Kerry, her brows knitted in worry, absentmindedly rubbed her wet hair with a towel. Lewis paced, swinging his arms back and forth impatiently. Hannah and Mack stood quietly together, his arm around her shoulders, her face drawn and white.

"Your friend's playing a joke on you," Mr. Tesch said when he came out. He was smiling. "C'mere, I'll show you."

They followed him back inside.

He stood in the center of the small room, pointing upward. "See those plastic panels up there?" He climbed up on the bench under the light, reached up and easily slid one of the lightweight panels sideways, revealing a large opening. "They're very lightweight," he said. "Slide in and out in a minute. The ducts up here lead all over the train. Your friend climbed up there and probably came down somewhere else, maybe in one of the compartments."

"No," Hannah said. "She wouldn't do that. Jean Marie wouldn't. Not ever, but especially not now. She would never scare us like this."

To her surprise, the detective took her seriously. "No? Doesn't have that kind of sense of humor?"

"No. She wouldn't think that was funny, worrying us. If she went up there, and I guess she must have, it was because someone made her do it."

The detective left the bench. "You hear anything while you were in the shower? Sounds of a struggle?"

Hannah shook her head. "No. Too much water running. I only heard Jean Marie's shower door click shut, that's all."

The man frowned. "Seems like you'd have heard someone pushing or pulling your friend up through the ceiling."

Not if she was unconscious, was Hannah's immediate reaction. "No one heard *me*," she said, "when I was being dragged to the baggage car. Whoever grabbed me made sure of that. He could have done the same thing to Jean Marie . . . covered her mouth so she couldn't make a sound."

He nodded. "Good point. All right, we'll get on it right away. Give me a description of the missing girl. And I want all of you to return to your compartments and stay there until I get back to you, okay?"

"We want to help look," Lewis said. "She's *our* friend. We can't just sit around and wait."

After giving that some thought, the detective nodded. "Fair enough. Divide up into groups and stay together, I insist on that. And get back to me if you see or hear anything. We'll find your friend, don't you worry."

When he had hurried away, Mack took charge, dividing the Parker High students into seven groups of four people each. "Spread out," he ordered. "Everybody take a different car. Wherever you find one of those ceiling panels, check that first. Climb up on something, lift the panel, and check it out. If you see *anything* you think you shouldn't, find Tesch and tell him."

Eugene was nowhere to be seen, but Dale asked, "So, if we find her, do we get a reward?" He grinned slyly. "Like maybe a date with the damsel in distress after we rescue her?"

Some people laughed, others tittered in embarrassment for Dale.

Everyone knew Jean Marie Westlake wouldn't be caught dead in the company of Dale Sutterworth, any more than she would have in Frog's company.

Hannah gasped at that thought. Caught *dead*? That no longer seemed like a harmless expression.

The search began.

Hannah pushed the wet hair back from her forehead as their group headed for the Observation Lounge to check it out. Kerry's hair was plastered down her back and had already soaked through her blouse. But she uttered not one word of complaint as they hurried through the cars.

Atta girl, Kerry, Hannah thought.

The Observation Lounge, all glass and sunshine,

was as empty as it had been when they awakened that morning. Everyone was out looking for Jean Marie.

Because the ceiling was mostly glass, there were no panels to check.

"Waste of time," Lewis muttered as they turned to leave. "Should have skipped this car." They all nodded in agreement, but at that very instant, a shrill scream split the air over their heads.

They stopped, frozen in their tracks.

Suddenly, a bright blur of hot pink sailed past the window in front of them, arcing downward like an arrow aimed at the ground, and disappeared.

Instinctively, Hannah's gaze shot to the ceiling glass and for just one tiny split-second, she thought she saw a movement overhead . . . the heel of a boot? Then it was gone, and there was nothing.

"What was *that*?" Lewis asked. "Something fell off the roof?"

Kerry turned to Hannah, her dark eyes fearful. "Pink . . ." she stammered, barely managing to squeeze out the words. "That pink . . . Jean Marie's robe . . ."

Hannah sucked in her breath. Jean Marie? No . . .

"We don't know that was her," Lewis said nervously, peering out the window.

Hannah stood up. "We can't wait to be sure," she said, her lips trembling. "The train's going too fast. We'll get too far away . . ."

Without hesitation, her arm shot up and her hand

closed around the emergency cord overhead. She yanked with great force.

Their ears rang with the agonizingly long, drawn-out scream of the train's wheels. After what seemed like an eternity, the train slowed and came to an angry halt.

Chapter 22

Hannah and her friends sat like statues, scarcely breathing, in the Observation Lounge where Ms. Quick had ordered them to wait for word on Jean Marie.

"I'm sure it wasn't her," she had said emphatically. "Maybe it was a scarf you saw, or even a newspaper blown by the wind."

A newspaper? A *pink* newspaper? Hannah shrank back against the seat then, biting her lower lip to keep from screaming, Just go find out! Hurry! Come back and tell me it wasn't Jean Marie, that she wasn't tossed off the roof of this train, tell me that! That's all I want to hear.

But when Ms. Quick returned, the conductor at her side, their faces told the story.

"I'm sorry," the teacher said softly, "I'm so sorry. Jean Marie is . . . is . . ." She couldn't continue.

Kerry screamed and Hannah's eyes filled with tears and the boys sat in mute disbelief, their hands in their laps.

"Mr. Dobbs is leaving the train now," Ms. Quick

added gently. "An ambulance is coming for . . . for Jean Marie, and he'll be going with it. We can't turn the train around, so we'll be going on to California. Those of you who want to leave the tour upon our arrival in San Francisco this afternoon may do so. The school is arranging plane transportation for anyone who wants it."

"And the detective?" Kerry asked bitterly, tears streaming down her cheeks, "what is *he* doing about this? I thought he came on the train to keep stuff like this from happening. Where *was* he when Jean Marie was thrown from the train?"

"Still looking for her. But none of us thought to look *outside* the train. Whoever did this must have taken Jean Marie up through the panels in the shower room and onto the roof of the train. He's on his way here now to ask you all a few more questions. I'd appreciate it if you'd be as helpful as possible."

Hannah could stand no more. Jumping up, she brushed past the adults and ran from the car. When Mack cried out at her to wait for him, she ignored his shout and kept going.

She ran all the way to the compartment. Sobs of grief and cries of anger rang from behind closed doors. The news about Jean Marie had spread quickly. But Hannah did not stop to talk to anyone. She needed desperately to be alone.

The compartment that had seemed so frightening yesterday — was that only yesterday? — seemed now warm and welcoming and private, so private. Let Mack and Lewis and Kerry answer Mr. Tesch's questions. She, for one, had no answers. None at all.

The very second they arrived in San Francisco, she was going to board a plane to Chicago, even if she was the only one who did.

I should have gone back when the train wheels told me to, she thought. I didn't listen, and I've been sorry ever since.

As Hannah reached her compartment, the train began moving again, quickly picking up speed, leaving behind the sound of the mournful ambulance wail as it arrived on the scene.

I will never see Jean Marie again, Hannah thought, and fresh tears filled her eyes.

When she opened the door, the compartment was dark, the window shade still pulled down from the day before. Hannah took a few steps and yanked the shade upward.

"Hello, Hannah," a voice said from behind her. "I thought you'd never get here."

Chapter 23

Hannah gasped and whirled, her back against the window, to find herself facing Lolly Slocum. She was dressed in boy's clothes — jeans, cowboy boots, plaid shirt and denim jacket — an outfit Frog had often worn. Her lank blonde hair was hidden under a worn felt cowboy hat.

She leaned against the door and smiled. "Hi, Hannah, how's it going? Not too well, I guess." She clucked her tongue sympathetically. "Too bad."

Hannah found her voice. "Lolly? You scared me half to death! What are you doing here? I thought you went home . . ."

"Went home?" The cowboy hat swung from side to side. "Not really. I told that idiot doctor I had motion sickness really bad. She was afraid I'd barf on her shiny black doctor's bag, so she found me a sleeping car and stashed me in a compartment and left me there. Or so she thought. Said she'd be back to check on me, but if she ever did come back, I was long gone. I just walked off that train and got back on this one. No problem." Then she added, in a confidential tone of voice, "I think that bag of hers was real leather, Hannah. Very fancy-schmancy."

Confused, Hannah frowned. "But . . . Ms. Quick heard from your family. They said you got back to Chicago okay."

"I sent that message myself, you twit!"

"You . . . you've been on the train this whole time? No . . . someone would have seen you."

"No one saw me because I didn't *want* them to. Not even Dale and Eugene. It would have spoiled everything." Lolly shrugged. "There are plenty of places to hide on this train."

Hannah's frown deepened, but along with her confusion a new feeling began to stir — an uneasiness, as if she were stepping up to the edge of a cliff and didn't dare look down for fear of getting dizzy. "You got back on the train but didn't tell anyone? You were . . . you were *hiding*?"

Lolly nodded and smirked with satisfaction. "Those ceiling panels in the shower room?"

Hannah thought of Jean Marie, and felt sick. "What about them?"

"They're in every rest room. Along with one of those little benches for people who are old or tired and have trouble bending to tie their shoes. Those benches are great for standing on to move the ceiling panel back, and then it's a cinch to hoist yourself up into the crawl space. It's not bad up there, not bad at all."

Hannah tried to speak and couldn't. She was

seeing Jean Marie plummeting to the dry, hard-baked desert floor from the roof of the train. Nausea threatened to overwhelm her.

Lolly's voice was light, teasing. "Feeling sick, Hannah? Your lovely trip hasn't been so lovely, has it?"

Fighting to stay calm, Hannah said, "Lolly, what are you doing here? You should be home or in a hospital. That noose around your neck . . ."

Lolly threw her head back and laughed. Sunshine streaming in through the unshaded window sent a gold, metallic shimmer into her pale blue eyes. "Oh, Hannah, don't be silly. I did that myself! When we went through the tunnel. Dale and Eugene never saw a thing. Too dark. They're not all that bright, anyway. If they heard anything, they never guessed it was me knotting that scarf around my poor little neck."

Hannah's jaw dropped. She stared, speechless.

"I'm good at knots. I worked on a boat one summer, to earn money." Her voice deepened, took on a note of harshness. "I didn't spend my summers vegging out around a pool, like you guys."

Hannah's face was a study in bewilderment. "You strangled yourself? Why? What for? I don't get it."

Lolly smiled again. "You will. Oh, you *will* get it, Hannah. Everything you deserve. Soon. But it wouldn't be any fun killing you without telling you why."

Killing? Hannah slid down onto one of the seats, her eyes on Lolly's face. "Lolly, what . . ."

"What, indeed?" Lolly laughed again, deeper and

harsher this time. An ugly sound. Looking at Hannah's hands she said, "You really did a number on your fingernails trying to get out of that coffin, didn't you?" And then she added with a sly grin, "You're not as lightweight as you look, Hannah. I had one heck of a time getting you into that baggage car."

When Hannah spoke, her voice came out thin and high-pitched. *"You?"*

Lolly nodded. "You bet! Too bad I missed any vital organs on your friend Lewis." Lolly shook her head regretfully. "I couldn't believe it when I saw him moving around the train a few hours later. I guess I'll just have to practice, practice, practice."

When Hannah didn't speak — because she couldn't — Lolly slapped her knee with her hand and laughed heartily. "Hannah, I wish you could have seen your face when you climbed onto that bunk. Or tried to. It was hilarious. Wish I'd had a video camera."

"You . . . you were there? When I saw . . . Frog?"

"Oh, Hannah, you're so dense! That wasn't him. How could it be? He's dead, thanks to you and your stupid, rotten friends! That was *me* in your bunk."

"But — how . . . ?"

"I wasn't in Drama Club for nothing. I wanted to act but that idiot Gruber wouldn't even give me the chance. Said I'd be perfect for makeup and hair." Lolly sneered in disgust. "Meaning I'd never appear on a stage while *she* was in charge. But . . ." the pale eyes glittered in triumph, "it came in handy after all, didn't it, Hannah? Doing the makeup, I mean. Didn't I look great as Roger — or *Frog* as you all called him? Come on," she said coaxingly, "admit it. I did a super job, right?"

Hannah wanted to stand up. She wanted to stand up and run from this calm, smiling, crazy person who had shut her in a coffin and tried to kill Lewis and . . .

"Mack?" she asked. "You locked Mack in that shed back in Denver?"

"Oh, big deal. I wanted to do something a lot worse, but I never got the chance. I was going to set it on fire. I thought it would be appropriate if Mack died the same way Roger did. But," Lolly sighed heavily, "too many people were passing back and forth at the entrance to the alley. I knew someone would save him.

"Speaking of your buddies, Hannah," Lolly continued, as friendly as if they were discussing a favorite class in school, "Kerry was supposed to find me in that upper berth, not you. I saw you guys tossing a coin in the train station — everyone was doing the same thing to decide who got the top bunk — and I could tell by the look on her face that she lost. Making myself look all burned and gross was aimed at her, not you." Her eyes narrowed. "The little witch. Roger told me how she treated him." Her voice softened, became dreamy, "He told me everything . . ."

"You were hiding in that upper berth all that time?"

"No, dummy! There's a ceiling panel right above it."

"But why?" Hannah whispered, "why are you doing this?"

Lolly snorted, her eyes cold. "Are you kidding? Roger is *dead*, Hannah. Dead! Gone forever! I loved him. And you were all so rotten to him. He didn't deserve that, Hannah. He was new and scared and he'd been dumped by his parents. He didn't deserve to be treated like pond scum."

Hannah hung her head. "We didn't know . . ." she murmured.

In one huge stride, Lolly was in front of her, bringing her arm up to whack Hannah on the side of the head with all her might. It lifted Hannah up and toppled her sideways. Her right ear and cheek cracked sharply against the wooden arm of the seat.

"Don't say you didn't know!" Lolly hissed, bending over Hannah. "You *should* have known! What kind of people *are* you?"

Then the anger seemed, suddenly, to drain out of her and she straightened up, saying sadly, "It doesn't matter. Roger is gone and I don't have anything without him. Dale and Eugene are losers." Then her face darkened and her eyes turned cold and hard as marbles. "But Roger died mad at me, Hannah, and that's *your* fault!"

"No, it's *not*!" Hannah said angrily. No one had ever hit her before in her life, and Lolly had hit her twice, on the back of the head that night, and now on her face. "Why did you kill Jean Marie?"

"Because Roger loved her." Lolly's pale eyes, no longer glittering with triumph, rested on Hannah's face. They were full of a terrible pain. "He really loved her. He only dated me because I was willing and Jean Marie wasn't." Lolly half-turned toward the window and looking out, said dully, "I hated Jean Marie more than I've ever hated anyone."

She isn't looking at me, Hannah thought, every nerve in her body on the alert. She's forgotten I'm here. She's off somewhere else, thinking about Jean Marie. I won't get another chance like this.

Moving like someone shot from a cannon, Hannah flew to her feet and threw herself at the door, unlatching it in one swift, sure motion. She was out in the hall and running before Lolly had even turned around.

Chapter 24

Hannah had fled the length of two cars when she pulled a door open and ran headlong into Mack. Kerry and Lewis were right behind him.

"Whoa!" Mack cried, reaching out to enfold her. "We were just coming to get you. You okay? I thought that detective would never let us leave." Then he drew her away from him and looked down into her face. "Hannah? What's wrong?"

"Lolly," Hannah gasped. She turned and pointed backward. "Lolly — back there . . . she — it's . . . it's Lolly — "

"Lolly?" Kerry echoed. "Hannah, Lolly got off the train. Remember?" Then, "Hannah, have you been napping? Did you have another nightmare?"

"No!" Hannah shouted. "It's *Lolly*! She killed Jean Marie! She told me. Come *on*!" And without waiting for an answer, she turned and began running back to the compartment.

Her friends followed, shaking their heads. Kerry muttered under her breath.

They ran into the conductor on their way and

Hannah insisted he come, too. "You have to arrest her," she babbled, her eyes feverish with intent. "You can do that, can't you? It's *your* train! She's a murderer, you have to arrest her. Get Mr. Tesch, *hurry*!"

Before the bewildered conductor could make sense of all that, Mr. Tesch called out to them from the doorway. He had been looking for Hannah to ask her the questions she'd skipped out on earlier.

"Hurry up," she cried urgently as they reached the compartment. "She's in here!"

She didn't wait for him to join them. Taking a deep breath, she slammed her palm down hard on the door latch and pushed the door open. "She's in here!" she cried, "Lolly's in here. You'll see that I wasn't dreaming."

But as the door swung open, a gust of hot, breathless desert air rushed toward them. It came from a huge, jagged hole in the window. The paisly curtains danced around it. The steady *ga-dink, ga-dink, ga-dink* of the wheels surged upward into the small space.

In one mass movement, they all piled inside, the conductor exclaiming in dismay over the ruined window. Hannah's eyes darted about the room, looking for signs of Lolly.

The room was empty.

"Hannah?" Kerry whispered, pointing. "Look at the mirror."

They all looked.

Slashed across the small rectangle of glass over

the sink, written in bright pink, which Hannah recognized as her own Pink Powderpuff lipstick, were the words:

I'LL BE WITH ROGER NOW.
I'M NOT SORRY FOR ANYTHING
L.

"Oh no!" the conductor breathed. "She threw herself out the window!"

A stunned silence filled the room, mixing with the hot air blasting in through the jagged hole. Slowly, carefully, they all moved as close to it as they dared. One by one, they looked out, expecting to see below them a dry desert floor. Instead, they found themselves gazing down upon a massive crevasse in the earth running for miles alongside the tracks. It was dry and hard and rocky on both sides and appeared to be bottomless.

"Lolly jumped into *that*?" Lewis whispered. "That — that canyon? She must have broken every bone in her body!"

A wisp of torn denim clung to one of the spikes of broken glass. The detective lifted it carefully, held it in his hand.

"She was wearing a denim jacket," Hannah told him.

Kerry's eyes fastened on the conductor. "Aren't you going to stop the train?"

He shook his head. "No point, Miss. We'd never find her down there. I'll put in a call to the local

Search and Rescue back there and give them the location. They'll find her." Then he sighed heavily and left. The detective went with him, promising Hannah he'd be back soon so she could fill him in on everything Lolly had told her.

"You won't be doing any harm by telling me," he pointed out gently, "now that she's dead."

"No," Hannah said softly when the two men had gone, "I don't believe it. She's playing another trick on us. She's hiding. And I know exactly where to look!"

Her friends stared at her as if they weren't sure they'd heard her correctly and hoped they hadn't.

"She *told* me," she explained, "she told me where she'd been hiding all that time." She ran to the upper berth, yanked it down from the wall. "In here." But there was no Lolly looking like Lolly and no Lolly madeup to look like Frog. Nothing.

An embarrassed silence filled the room. "Hannah — " Mack began, but she interrupted him.

"No, no, look, . . . okay, so she's not in there. There are other places — she hid all over the train. Please, we *have* to find her. If we don't, she'll come back and hurt more people. Me — or Mack — she was so angry — "

"I'll help you look," Mack said gently, taking her arm. "Lewis? Kerry?"

Hannah saw the look he gave them, knew it meant, humor her, she's upset. She didn't care. As long as they helped her look for Lolly, it didn't matter *why*.

The search took all afternoon. Every time one of them wanted to give up, Hannah insisted they continue, her voice cracking with anxiety, her eyes burning with determination. "We'll *find* her, I know we will! We have to keep looking."

While they searched, she told them everything that Lolly had said. Kerry was skeptical at first, but Hannah's voice had a ring of truth to it and eventually, it all made sense.

"Did you find out where she put Frog while you were in the coffin?" Lewis asked.

Hannah shook her head. "No. There wasn't time. But when we find her, I'm going to make her tell me."

But they didn't find Lolly.

When Lewis and Kerry stopped to eat something, Hannah refused to join them. "I haven't checked the ceiling in Kitty Winn's compartment yet. You go ahead." They eyed her nervously, but they left.

Mack stayed with her the whole time. He seemed to sense that this was something she had to do, and for that she was grateful.

They found nothing, no sign of Lolly beyond two wrinkled candy wrappers in one of the crawl spaces and a blue comb with two broken teeth in another.

At four o'clock, Lewis and Kerry caught up with them to warn Hannah that they had less than an hour before arriving in California. "We're supposed to get our things together," she said carefully.

"We're going to be leaving the train, Hannah, and all of this terrible stuff will be over."

"Yeah," Lewis added, his gray eyes sympathetic as he looked at Hannah, "and Lolly's gone, Hannah. We proved that, right? Are you still going to fly back home right away?"

Hannah nodded wearily. She was so tired her body felt like rubber. Her head ached. "I just want to go home," she said quietly. "I'm sorry I made you waste your afternoon. You were right. I just didn't want to believe she'd jumped. I should have known. She sounded so sad, so hopeless and she missed Frog so much . . ."

Giving up the futile search, they rested in their compartments during the last hour of the trip.

It was a strange group of teenagers that left the train. People waiting in the train station stared at them: twenty-eight teenagers not making a sound other than soft murmurs. A sight not seen every day.

Hannah, climbing slowly down the metal steps, turned her head to give the train one last, bleak look. She had endured the most horrifying moments of her life, shut up in a dark and airless box, on that train. Lewis had been stabbed. Jean Marie . . . Jean Marie was dead. And Lolly had committed suicide.

She watched with tears in her eyes as several porters unloaded Frog's coffin. I hate Lolly for killing Jean Marie, she thought, but she was right about one thing. We *were* mean to Frog. And it was my guilty conscience that wanted to think he was still alive.

Now they were both dead . . . Frog *and* Lolly.

She saw Dale and Eugene emerge from the train. Both looked thoroughly shaken by Lolly's suicide. Their eyes were clouded, their shoulders slumped. They looked lost and lonely.

The tour group entered the big bus to San Francisco quietly and solemnly.

But during the twenty-minute ride to San Francisco from Oakland, the mood began to change. When they crossed the bridge, windows were opened to allow the fresh, cool, salty air in. It was invigorating, and slowly, gradually, conversation began, a word at a time. Then there was a bit of laughter here and there, and people began craning their necks to see. Little by little, the tension and gloom evaporated like San Francisco fog.

By the time they reached the city and disembarked, the mood had changed to one of excitement and eagerness.

Even Hannah, looking out upon the tall buildings and the choppy waters of the sun-streaked Bay, began to feel her spirits lift.

Mack came up to her outside the Transbay Terminal and said, "I just talked to Ms. Quick. Your plane doesn't leave for three hours, so we thought you might spend them sightseeing with us." Hannah surprised all of them, especially herself, by saying, "Okay. Why not?"

Mack, Lewis, and Kerry stared at her.

"Really?" Kerry squeaked. "You'll come?"

Hannah laughed. "Yes. I've never seen San Francisco, I've never seen the ocean or even a bay and I'm not going to sit here all by myself for three hours. Yes, I'll come. Besides," she added softly, "Jean Marie would want us to do this."

Mack smiled at her and took her hand.

Chapter 25

The place Mack had in mind was called Rockview.

"I read about it," he told Hannah as he led her to the waiting bus. "It's a big old house up on a hill looking out over the water. If we get lucky, we'll see sea lions on the rocks. And if it's too foggy, there's a restaurant and a gift shop upstairs and an arcade downstairs. You can do a lot in a place like that in three hours."

Hannah knew Mack was trying to help her forget everything that happened. She gave him another smile, and he squeezed her hand. Hannah was glad to be off the train, but she knew that memories of that horrible ride would haunt her for a long time to come.

If only Jean Marie could be with them . . .

It wasn't foggy at Rockview when they arrived. But during dinner in the warm, cozy restaurant overlooking the water, they were able to watch in awe as the thick, white cloud appeared and rolled toward them, banishing everything in its path. The distant lights of huge ships out on the water disappeared, smaller boats vanished, even the great brown rocks closer to shore were swallowed up in one quick gulp.

"Weird," Kerry said softly, her fork halfway to her mouth. "It's like a steamroller . . . but it looks so soft and fluffy."

"Now you see it, now you don't," Lewis said, peering through the big picture window into what was now an unbroken blanket of gray-white mist. "I guess we can forget about the sea lions. We can't even see the *rocks*."

By the time they went downstairs to visit the arcade, darkness had enveloped the concrete walkway on three sides of the house, all facing the water.

Because the thick fog had robbed them of any view, they entered the arcade, noisy with calliope music and laughter and thick with bodies. Almost immediately, Hannah became separated from her friends but, rather than being upset, she was grateful. Now she was free to go outside alone. She felt as if she'd been cooped up forever, first on the train, then on the bus. She needed fresh air, even if it was foggy and drizzly.

Without telling anyone she was leaving, Hannah pushed her way through the crowd and went outside to the seawall overlooking the water. Except for the lights shining out from the arcade and the restaurant above them, it was dark, and very cold. Drizzle from the fog moistened her face and lips. It felt very refreshing after the stuffiness of the arcade.

A large section of the stone wall protecting viewers had crumbled into the cold, choppy water. The destroyed area was roped off with a sign reading:

DANGER
DO NOT ENTER

But it was easy to avoid that area. The earlier sightseers had disappeared, leaving the evening chill for the warmth of the arcade or restaurant and gift shop. The walkway was hers alone.

Grateful for the solitude, Hannah moved close to the wall, peering over the edge to watch the pounding surf below her. She felt she would like to remain there forever, watching the powerful, rushing tide collide with the rocks, the resulting foamy spray dancing high up in the air, almost close enough to touch. She licked her lips and tasted saltwater.

Hannah leaned over the protective stone wall and let the sight and sound of the roaring waves crashing against the huge rocks below soothe her shattered nerves.

Mack's right, she thought. It's all over now. She knew that the sadness she felt for Frog and Lolly and especially for poor Jean Marie would remain with her for a long time to come. But slowly, slowly, for the first time since she'd boarded the train, Hannah could feel herself beginning to relax. I should go in and join my friends for the little while I have left here, Hannah thought. Mack will be happy to see me.

She was about to turn around and head for the arcade when an arm fastened itself around her neck and a voice she recognized instantly said softly, "Hi, Hannah. Fancy meeting you here."

The voice belonged to Lolly Slocum.

Chapter 26

"I have a knife," Lolly whispered. Something cold and metallic pressed against Hannah's ear. "Make even the tiniest sound and you'll never make another."

"Don't," Hannah begged when she could speak. "Please, don't. . . ."

Lolly began pulling Hannah sideways, yanking cruelly at her neck. It hurt, but Hannah didn't cry out. She was afraid to.

"Where . . . where were you?" Hannah whispered. "When we were looking for you? We looked everywhere."

"You didn't look everywhere," Lolly said with contempt. "Not in the coffin."

They were scuttling sideways, toward the roped-off area. Laughter and music rang out from the arcade. Hannah fixed her frightened eyes on the windows, trying to will Mack to realize she was missing and come rescue her. But in that crowd . . . would he even realize she was gone?

They reached the rope. Lolly ducked underneath and roughly pulled Hannah with her.

She isn't going to stab me, Hannah thought with rising nausea. She doesn't have to. All she has to do is push me over that broken wall. I'll be smashed to bits on the rocks below.

The roaring surf no longer seemed comforting.

Stall, stall, Hannah ordered herself. Keep her talking until Mack or Lewis or Kerry realizes you're not in the arcade. Keep her talking . . .

So she asked the question that had been torturing her. "Lolly," she said in a trembling voice as Lolly dragged her backward, closer and closer to the crumbled wall and that deadly roar, "if you were hiding in the coffin, where was Frog? Did you . . . did you *move* him?"

Lolly's laughter pealed out into the thick mist, as if slicing it down the middle. "Oh, Hannah, he isn't in that coffin! He never was." Backing Hannah up against the broken wall, Lolly released her grip but stood blocking Hannah's way, an immovable bulk.

She held something up in front of Hannah. The faint glow from the arcade bounced off the metal object she was holding. It wasn't a knife. It was, Hannah realized, peering through the darkness at it, a tin canister, short and squat.

"This," Lolly said triumphantly, "is *Frog*!"

Drizzle coated Hannah's hair and slid down her cheeks. Behind her she could hear the hungry pounding of the waves waiting to swallow her up.

“Frog?” was all Hannah could manage as she stared at the canister. “Frog?”

Lolly nodded. “You don’t think anyone cared enough about him to provide a real funeral for him, do you? Too much bother to have him sent home to be buried. They had him cremated!”

“Frog was never in the coffin? Then why was it on the train?”

Lolly grinned. “I ordered it. I’m having it sent COD to his parents. As a reminder. That they had a son they didn’t want, not when he was alive and not when he was dead. They’ll get a call from the railroad station and they’ll come down to see what they’re getting and there it will be . . . their son’s coffin. Only he won’t be in it. They won’t care about that, but they sure will be ticked off when they’re given the shipping invoice.” Lolly giggled with relish.

“How . . . how did you get his ashes?” Mack, where are you? Hannah thought desperately. Why aren’t you looking for me?

“*They* didn’t care. But I knew exactly what to do with them.” Lolly lifted her head, gazed around her. “So they gave them to me. San Francisco was one of his favorite places. He used to talk about it all the time. I knew about the tour, and I knew it wasn’t too late to sign up. It would be perfect. I’d bring him back here, where he loved to be, and I’d take care of you guys at the same time. And the great thing about the empty coffin was, I knew it would make a great hiding place.” She held up the canister again, shoving it in Hannah's face.

And Hannah saw the tattoo. The winged rat, its fangs bared, exactly like the one Frog had, and in the same place — on Lolly's left wrist.

"That was *you* in the coffin," Hannah said. "But . . . if we'd opened the lid all the way . . ."

"You would have seen exactly what you saw in the berth," Lolly said confidently. "And you thought *that* was Roger, didn't you? I put the makeup on before I climbed into the coffin every time. Just in case. No one would have known I wasn't Roger. I mean," she said with a chuckle, "it's not as though they'd look too closely, know what I mean?

"It's funny," she added then with an evil grin, "that you and Roger are going to end up in the same place, after all. Don't you think that's funny? He always wanted to hang around you guys. I never understood why, considering the way you treated him. We fought about it. A terrible fight." Tears of pain filled her small, pale eyes. "And I never got a chance to say I was sorry. He didn't want me there that night, the night he died . . . I knew that. He wanted to be with Jean Marie. But I showed up anyway, pulled up right behind him when he parked. He was furious when he saw me. But I knew he'd need me when he got hurt. And he *did* get hurt, didn't he, Hannah? Who would know that better than you?"

Then all the fight seemed to go out of her and she added sadly, "But he wouldn't let me take care of him then. He was hurt and angry and he pushed me away when I tried to comfort him." Suddenly, her head flew up and the sadness was replaced again by fresh anger. "*Your* fault, Hannah, all *your* fault!"

Hannah's hands were behind her, trying to keep her body from touching the crumbling wall. One hand reached out tentatively, groping, searching for a piece of loose rock, or a piece of the crumbling wall. At last she found one, and grasped it tightly in her right hand.

"You know, Hannah," Lolly went on confidently, her voice low and sinister, "if the fall doesn't kill you, I've heard there are man-eating fish in these waters. In a couple of days, you're not going to look so pretty — "

The movement was so swift and sudden that Lolly never saw Hannah's arm dart out from behind her back. The chunk of concrete caught her directly above the left temple with as much force as Hannah could muster.

As Lolly reacted, Hannah bent forward and leapt sideways, to crouch, hands over her mouth, on the solid side of the wall.

Lolly grunted in surprise as the rock struck her. One arm flew to her head. But the other arm, the one that had been displaying the canister close to Hannah's face, jerked in a reflex action as the rock hit its target. The involuntary movement sent the canister spurting out of Lolly's hand. It flew up, up, and out over the edge of the crumbling wall.

It was about to begin its descent to the roaring surf when Lolly, with a desperate cry, lunged for it, both arms outstretched.

She caught it.

But to do so, she had to throw her body, full force, against the broken wall.

The crumbling concrete gave way, disintegrating completely under the force of Lolly's strong body.

Still clutching the canister, Lolly plunged forward and plumeted to the rocks and crashing waves below.

Chapter 27

At the very moment that Lolly plunged into the sea, someone called Hannah's name. She heard nothing. Crouched in a wet, miserable little ball against the concrete wall and lost in shock and horror, she was deaf to everything but the roar of the water beneath her as the huge, hungry waves swallowed up Lolly Slocum.

She covered her face with her hands.

"Hannah! Hannah, it's okay! It's okay now!"

She lifted her head. "Mack?"

He reached down and gently pulled her to her feet. She sagged against him, clutching, hugging, so glad to be safe.

Kerry and Lewis were with Mack. "What happened, Hannah?" Kerry asked, patting Hannah's shoulder.

"Lolly . . ." she whispered.

Lewis nodded. "We thought it was Frog when we spotted the two of you from the arcade window. Then her hair fell out of that cap she was wearing and we knew who it was. We ran to get out of there but it took us forever. No one would let us through."

"It's my fault," Kerry said quietly. "I should have made sure you were with me. I didn't realize we'd been separated until I turned around and you weren't there. I thought you were playing video games with Mack and Lewis until Mack showed up and asked me where you were."

"Let's go inside, Hannah," Mack said, leading her away from the viewing area. "You're soaked and you're shivering."

"I don't want to go into the arcade. All those people . . ."

They went to the restaurant instead. It was nearly empty and they sat at a table in the corner. While the others ordered, Mack went to call the police, and Ms. Quick.

"Lolly didn't jump from the train, after all?" Kerry asked when they'd been served with cups of steaming hot coffee.

Hannah shook her head. Mack had made her exchange her wet sweater for his dry one, but her damp hair chilled the back of her neck and her skin felt salty and sticky. "No. She was hiding again."

"I don't get it," Lewis said, shaking his head. "Did Frog's death unhinge her or what? What was she trying to do?"

Hannah leaned back against her chair and closed her eyes. "Get even," she said quietly.

Mack returned and said the police were on their way, as was Ms. Quick.

"Get even for what?" Kerry asked sharply. "Jean

Marie never did anything mean to Lolly. She wouldn't have."

"Not to Lolly. To Frog. All those things we talked about in the Cafe that day . . ."

"But not you, Hannah. You didn't say anything. And you're the one she tried to kill tonight."

Hannah took a sip of coffee, grateful for its warmth. "I didn't say anything," she said quietly, setting her cup back in its saucer, "because I was too ashamed. What I did to Frog was worse than any of the rest of you." Her cheeks deepened in color. "But I'm going to tell you now.

"It was all because of my party," she began, slipping back in her memory . . .

Her father wanted help with the yard work before her party, so he hired Frog. Every day for a week he was there, trimming bushes, mowing, weeding the flower beds, pruning the trees. He worked hard, Hannah had to admit.

She felt sorry for him, so she brought him cold lemonade when he was stringing the colored lights across the lawn. Turned the sprinkler on to cool him off when he was sweating in the hot sun over a flower bed. Fixed a sandwich and some fruit to take to him when he was struggling with the heavy recycling bins her father wanted moved.

It just seemed like the decent thing to do.

"Some bash you're giving here, huh?" he said one hot afternoon when she was sitting at the patio table folding napkins. "The whole school coming or what?"

"Just about," she answered.

"Figured," was all he said.

Hannah couldn't help thinking how awful it must be to be disliked by so many people. Okay, it was his own fault. He could have tried harder to be nice. But she also couldn't help wondering how many people had really given him a chance. The new kid in town . . . hadn't they all judged him pretty quickly?

And he was right about one thing: practically the whole school was coming to this party, the biggest she'd ever given. And he had worked so hard to make the grounds look pretty and nice. . . . One day it just slipped out, before she had time to consider what she was doing, what her friends would say.

Frog had said, for the hundredth time, "I guess just about everybody's coming to this thing, huh?" and that was when she did it. The words slid out of her mouth as easily as if they'd been buttered: "You can come, too, if you want."

Immediately, instantly, they both knew she regretted releasing the awful words.

And they both knew it was too late. She couldn't take it back, and there was no way he wasn't going to come.

Hannah wrestled with it every second of the next few days before the party. Her friends would have a fit when he walked in. No one could stand him. Several of the boys he'd had fistfights with would be there. Kerry would be appalled.

What was I thinking? she screamed at herself. He doesn't belong at this party. He doesn't know anyone, he won't have any fun. Everyone will be mad at me. It'll ruin everything if he shows up.

And she knew he would show up. There was no way he wouldn't. The look on his face when those dreadful words slipped out of her mouth had been the same look her brother Tad wore on his face when he finally got the Nintendo he'd prayed for.

He'd come, all right.

And the party she'd planned for so long would become a total disaster.

Hannah was a nervous wreck that night. She paced back and forth in the front hall in her expensive new party dress of deep forest green and her high heels, wearing her mother's jade earrings, with her hair curled up high on her head. She smiled at her guests as they began arriving and directed them toward the food, and when someone came to her and asked where a particular CD was, she told him, smiling, smiling all the while even though her stomach was churning and her teeth kept clenching and unclenching.

Because, how could she possibly allow Frog at her party? How could she let him ruin it?

The invitation had slipped out on an impulse. And it was retrieved in the same way.

When Hannah looked through the front window and saw him get out of his car and start across the street, it was as if her body took over and moved her outside, quickly, quickly, closing the door behind her, standing with her back against it, the sentry at the gate forbidding entry to the new unwanted — oh, so unwanted! — guest.

She hardly saw Lolly tagging along behind him, calling his name.

He was wearing what she was positive was a brand-new sport coat, and his longish hair was slicked down. He walked up the steps with an excited bounce. Lolly, hurrying along behind him, was wearing a ghastly purple dress with huge puffed sleeves.

"Hi," he said with a huge smile.

I can't do this, she thought with certainty, I can't.

But she did.

When they got to the door, Hannah said in a low, pained voice, "I'm really sorry, but the party's been cancelled. I'm not feeling well . . . the flu, I think, I've got this terrible headache and my stomach . . . well, I hate to do it, but I have to send everyone home. I was just about to when you came."

Music and laughter rang out behind them, coming, it seemed to Hannah, from each tiny crevice between the red bricks, through every window, beneath every door.

"Sick?" Frog said, disbelieving. "You don't look sick. You look," he flushed and lowered his head, "you look beautiful."

Hannah did feel sick, then. "Thanks, but I really feel awful. And if it's the flu, I don't want to give it to anyone else, right? I'm really sorry, after all that hard work you did. Maybe I can have the party next week."

The look on Frog's face then would haunt Hannah for a long time.

Without another word, he turned and ran down the steps, leaving Lolly behind. He jumped into his car and roared off, tires screeching, not even waiting to see if Hannah's guests really were leaving.

From somewhere far, far away, Hannah was vaguely aware of Lolly's voice shrieking after the speeding car, "See? Didn't I tell you? Didn't I?"

"He didn't have to wait to see if everyone else left," Hannah finished her story, "because he knew no one would be leaving. He knew I was lying."

Her friends knew the rest of the story. Five minutes later, after Lolly had left, her head held as high as she could manage, Frog had crashed his car into a brick wall at high speed.

"We heard the sirens," Hannah reminded them, "but we never gave it a thought. We were all having too much fun."

They sat in silence for several minutes. Then Hannah said softly, "I didn't know Lolly and Frog had fought about it. She didn't want him to come to the party because she knew that . . . we . . . really didn't want them there and that something bad would happen. She was right, wasn't she? And that made him even madder, finding out that she'd been right all along. He was furious with her when he drove off. It must have just about killed her, not straightening things out with him before he died.

"But it wasn't her fault. It was *mine.*" Hannah's breath caught in a sob. "And I've been sorry ever since, but what good does that do either of them?"

"Hannah," Mack said finally, "it's over. It's all over now. We were *all* crummy to the guy, and to Lolly, too, and we're all sorry."

"And now we should forget it," Kerry said firmly. "We'll never forget Jean Marie. But, like Mack said, it's over. Finally."

"No," Hannah said softly, lifting her head, her eyes full of regret. "I don't want to forget it. I don't want any of us to forget it. If we do, what's the point?"

"So you're still going home?" Lewis asked.

Hannah thought about it. She was here, in a wonderful, exciting city, with friends she cared about and trusted. Lolly was gone now. So was Frog. Would going back home change anything that had happened? Would it be wrong to stay?

"No," she said. "I'm not going home. I'm staying."

They all smiled.

"But," she added, taking Mack's hand in hers, "I'm not going to forget, either. And tomorrow, while Kerry's shopping, I'm coming back here, to Rockview, to see the ocean in the sunshine. I'm coming back to say a decent good-bye to Lolly and Frog. Then it will really be over."

And Mack said, "I'll come with you."

Kerry and Lewis nodded. "We will, too."

And Kerry added with a grin, "and *then* we'll go shopping."

About the Author

"Writing tales of horror makes it hard to convince people that I'm a nice, gentle person," says DIANE HOH. "I love rainbows and wildflowers and butterflies and babies, and I wouldn't swat a fly unless it was diving directly into my fruit salad.

"So what's a nice woman like me doing scaring people?

"Having the time of my life. Discovering the fearful side of life: what makes the heart pound, the adrenaline flow, the pulse throb, the breath catch in the throat. And hoping always that the reader is having a frightfully good time, too."

Diane Hoh grew up in Warren, Pennsylvania, "a lovely small town on the Allegheny River." Since then, she has lived in New York, Colorado, and North Carolina, before settling in Austin, Texas, where she plans to stay. "Reading and writing take up most of my life," says Hoh, "along with family, music, and gardening." Her horror novels include: *Funhouse*, *The Accident*, *The Invitation*, and *The Fever*.

THE BABYSITTERS CLUB

Need a babysitter? Then call the Babysitters Club. Kristy Thomas and her friends are all experienced sitters. They can tackle any job from rampaging toddlers to a pandemonium of pets. To find out all about them, read on!

The Babysitters Club No 1:
Kristy's Great Idea
The Babysitters Club No 2:
Claudia and the Phantom Phone Calls
The Babysitters Club No 3:
The Truth About Stacey
The Babysitters Club No 4:
Mary Anne Saves The Day
The Babysitters Club No 5:
Dawn and the Impossible Three
The Babysitters Club No 6:
Kristy's Big Day
The Babysitters Club No 7:
Claudia and Mean Janine
The Babysitters Club No 8:
Boy Crazy Stacey
The Babysitters Club No 9:
The Ghost at Dawn's House
The Babysitters Club No 10:
Logan Likes Mary Anne!
The Babysitters Club No 11:
Kristy and the Snobs
The Babysitters Club No 12:
Claudia and the New Girl
The Babysitters Club No 13:
Goodbye Stacey, Goodbye
The Babysitters Club No 14:
Hello, Mallory
The Babysitters Club No 15:
Little Miss Stoneybrook . . . and Dawn
The Babysitters Club No 16:
Jessi's Secret Language
The Babysitters Club No 17:

Mary Anne's Bad Luck Mystery
The Babysitters Club No 18:
Stacey's Mistake
The Babysitters Club No 19:
Claudia and the Bad Joke
The Babysitters Club No 20:
Kristy and the Walking Disaster
The Babysitters Club No 21:
Mallory and the Trouble with Twins
The Babysitters Club No 22:
Jessi Ramsey, Pet-sitter
The Babysitters Club No 23:
Dawn on the Coast
The Babysitters Club No 24:
Kristy and the Mother's Day Surprise
The Babysitters Club No 25:
Mary Anne and the Search for Tigger
The Babysitters Club No 26:
Claudia and the Sad Goodbye

Look out for:

The Babysitters Club No 27:
Jessi and the Superbrat
The Babysitters Club No 28:
Welcome Back, Stacey
The Babysitters Club No 29:
Mallory and the Mystery Diary
The Babysitters Club No 30:
Mary Anne and the Great Romance
The Babysitters Club No 31:
Dawn's Wicked Stepsister
The Babysitters Club No 32:
Kristy and the Secret of Susan

THE UNDERWORLD TRILOGY
Peter Beere

When life became impossible for the homeless of London many left the streets to live beneath the earth. They made their homes in the corridors and caves of the Underground. They gave their home a name. They called it UNDERWORLD.

UNDERWORLD
It was hard for Sarah to remember how long she'd been down there, but it sometimes seemed like forever. It was hard to remember a life on the outside. It was hard to remember the real world. Now it seemed that there was nothing but creeping on through the darkness, there was nothing but whispering and secrecy.

And in the darkness lay a man who was waiting to kill her . . .

UNDERWORLD II
"Tracey," she called quietly. No one answered. There was only the dark threatening void which forms Underworld. It's a place people can get lost in, people can disappear in. It's not a place for young girls whose big sisters have deserted them. Mandy didn't know what to do. She didn't know what had swept her sister and her friends from Underworld. All she knew was that Tracey had gone off and left her on her own.

UNDERWORLD III
Whose idea was it? Emma didn't know and now it didn't matter anyway. It was probably Adam who had said, "Let's go down and look round the Underground." It was something to tell their friends about, something new to try. To boast that they had been inside the secret Underworld, a place no one talked about, but everyone knew was there.

It had all seemed like a great adventure, until they found the gun . . .

Also by Peter Beere

CROSSFIRE

When Maggie runs away from Ireland, she finds herself roaming the streets of London destitute and alone. But Maggie has more to fear then the life of a runaway. Her step-father is an important member of the IRA – and if he doesn't find her before his enemies do, Maggie might just find herself caught up in the crossfire . . .